RISING DARKNESS

SHADOW CITY: SILVER WOLF

JEN L. GREY

CHAPTER ONE

M y body bounced, causing my restrained wrists to
move and burn.

What the...

I attempted to open my eyes, but my head lolled to the
side as my body jarred again. Heat surrounded me with the
faint stench of exhaust, making my head swim even more. If
I didn't know any better, I would think I was drunk or had
lost a lot of blood, but that couldn't have happened. I'd been
in the coffee shop just a few minutes ago...

Griffin, my fated mate, linked, *Sterlyn. Please tell me
you're awake.*

Wow, he'd called me by my real name. *I like you saying
my name.* He'd always called me Dove before we'd become
mates.

Oh, thank God. Griffin sounded relieved. *Where
are you?*

The question nudged me to focus a little more. I pried
my eyes open and took in the dimness around me. At first, I
saw double, but slowly, my brain filtered the picture into
one. Gray upholstery was smashed against my face and

silver metal outlined the ceiling, which was about a foot above me.

Holy shit. This was the kind of nightmare I'd had as a child. *I'm in the trunk of a car.*

What? he growled. *I'm going to kill whoever did this to you.*

Not if I got to them first. I took a deep breath, trying to get my head on straight. The first task I needed to address was getting my wrists unbound. Luckily, Griffin had gotten some guards to run to the store and purchase me some shirts and a few pairs of jeans, so I had my security measure strapped to my ankle.

I turned on my side, bending my legs as far back as they could go. While I was growing up, part of my alpha training regimen had included daily stretching, so I was more flexible than most wolves. Something my father had drilled into me from birth.

In the eyes of male alphas, I already had one disadvantage just by being a woman, so I had to be stronger, better, and faster than all of them.

Sexism was real—especially in the supernatural world. Unfortunately, I had no pack to lead because they'd all been slaughtered, not even a month ago.

But that didn't mean I'd give up. My mother had taught me better than that.

My fingers fumbled on the handle of my knife, and at this odd angle, the rope dug into my wrists even more.

At least, the pain helped clear my head. I inhaled, enduring the sting of the rope, and managed to pull the knife from the sheath. My best friend growing up, Zoe, had always teased me about carrying the knife everywhere—but the habit had served me well, especially during the past few weeks.

Are you hurt? Griffin asked, as misery laced his words.

Getting the knife's sharp edge onto the rope proved difficult, between the jarring from the road and the awkward placement of my hands. *No, not really. They drugged me with something that's still affecting me. How long have I been gone?*

About an hour. You linked me with "Help," and when I got to the coffee shop, Carter was frantic and told me that someone took you. Whoever it was drug you out the back door, and then your scent disappeared.

At his words, something tickled the back of my mind, but I was at a loss as to what. Either way, the car had to have been waiting for me. After we'd been attacked yesterday by the men who'd murdered my pack, and we'd killed everyone, I hadn't expected them to strike again so soon. But someone had come back to capture me.

My skin rubbed against the rope, and blood dripped down my hands, making it difficult to keep a good grip on the knife. If I didn't get out of here, I'd be rolling up to God knew where, and my chance of escaping would be greatly reduced. *Carter asked me to grab some coffee beans, and that's the last thing I remember.* I felt like there was more to recall...but I couldn't access the memory.

Someone had gotten the drop on me—which shouldn't have been possible—and the encounter was a blur. That had to be due to whatever had knocked my ass out.

Gritting my teeth, I continued to saw at the rope and, after what felt like an eternity, it began to loosen. *My hands are almost free.*

Do you have any clue where you're going? Griffin sighed. *Rosemary is looking for you, but we don't know where to search. Killian went north, and I'm heading south.*

I'll get you some sort of location in a second. I was

getting my ass out of here. I wasn't going to wait for one of them to find me—they might not be able to. From the rhythm of the car, whoever was driving was going the speed limit and not driving wildly, which meant there probably weren't any visible signs that he'd kidnapped someone.

When I cut through the last bit of rope, I came damn near close to crying. I placed the knife beside me and flexed my wrists, trying to get some circulation back. They were raw but would heal quickly on their own.

After wiping the blood onto my pants, I searched for the emergency release. My gaze landed on a white handle that had arrows pointing to pull right to open.

Griffin linked, *What do you mean, you're going to get a location?*

I'm jumping out. The closer I got to wherever they were taking me, the less chance I'd have to get free.

Are you insane? Griffin growled. *You're going to get hurt.*

If I don't, I'll wind up wherever they want me, which could be worse. He wasn't trying to be an asshole; we were newly mated. On top of that, he wasn't trained in battle strategy. But dammit, that was something he'd need to rectify, and soon, now that he was with me. Unfortunately, people had found out my kind—the silver wolves—still existed, and they had come after me. We had to find out who "they" were and neutralize them, because the thought of living my entire life on the run didn't sit well with me.

Not wasting another second, I placed my knife back in its sheath and grabbed the release. I gathered my wits because, as soon as this trunk opened, the driver and whoever else might be in the car would know. At least the driver would be in human form and not animal; I only prayed they didn't have any guns.

The only way to know what I was up against was to go through with the plan, so I yanked the release, and the trunk cracked open. Wind blew inside, whipping my long silver hair into my face. I pulled it to one side and looked out of the trunk.

There wasn't a car right behind me, so at least there was that. If I had to jump out, I wouldn't be playing Frogger, trying not to get hurt. The area was thick with trees, and we were driving on a two-lane road. My captors were either avoiding the interstate or taking me to some backwoods area. Or both. *There's a county road sign.* I read off the numbers to him.

You're going south, but more important—how the hell do you know that? Griffin growled. *Please, don't do anything stupid.*

I decided to stop overthinking and go for it. I pushed the trunk all the way open, and the car swerved. *I'm jumping out now.*

No—don't, he said, sounding frantic. *Just wait for one of us to catch up with you.* A whirlwind of emotions slammed into me. He was scared and felt helpless.

It's too late. The tires squealed as the driver slowed down. *They already know I'm escaping.*

I wanted to shut down the bond between us, but I couldn't do that to him. If I'd been in his shoes, I wouldn't have been much better off, and it wouldn't be right to worry him more than he already was. But I had to ignore his emotions and focus on escape.

The car was almost at a complete stop, so I jumped out and rolled to prevent injury. I jumped up and ran to the tree line, hoping to hide and see what I was up against.

Pushing my legs as hard as they would go, I raced toward a tree with a large enough trunk and vibrant new spring leaves to keep me hidden for a moment. I welcomed the adrenaline pumping through me, partially clearing my head of whatever they'd injected me with. I flung myself behind the tree trunk then peeked my head around toward the road.

Lurching, the car came to a stop, leaving gray smoke rising from beneath the tires. The driver's side door opened, and a tall, muscular man jumped out. He was almost as large as my dad with dark, cinnamon-colored hair.

He had to be a bear shifter, which didn't sit well with me. All of the attackers in the group we'd recently faced down had been wolves, except for one crow, and now this guy. Unless the bear who'd attacked me in a bar in town not long ago was connected with them too.

So many races being involved in this scheme complicated matters. That meant that multiple races that usually were divided were working together, which happened only when the enemy of their enemy was their friend. Did that mean they were working together to eliminate or control the last remaining silver wolf? I didn't like the implications.

"You aren't going to get away," the guy bellowed, his bear growl bleeding through his words. "So why don't you come out now and make it easier on the both of us?"

I rolled my eyes. Did he think that would actually work?

He sniffed, catching my scent. His eyes focused right where I was hiding.

That hadn't taken long, but I hadn't expected it to. At least I knew that he was alone, which struck me as odd.

"How did you wake up so fast?" He sneered as he strolled toward me, placing his hands in his pockets as if he didn't have a care in the world.

But he wasn't fooling me. I could feel the tension rolling off his body. He wanted to appear confident to try to make me nervous. Maybe I should play the game right back at him. "Not sure." I stepped out from behind the tree and forced a smile. "Maybe you didn't use enough."

My casual demeanor must have hit the mark because he paused. Instead of him throwing me off guard, I'd managed to do it to him.

"Well, it doesn't matter now." He gestured to the car. "Let's get going, and you won't have to be hurt again."

"Can I sit in front?" I smiled, but my body was coiled, ready to fight.

We both knew how this would end. Right now, we were playing some stupid game of who was the most dominant.

"No, but I'll let you choose the music."

"Going to have to say no." I took a few steps toward him, wanting to get this done. I was so damn tired of fighting.

"Then I'm going to have to insist." He marched forward but stopped about ten feet from me. "Now."

"Good luck with that." I spread my legs and got into a fighter's stance.

"You think you can take me?" He chuckled, but there was an edge to it. "I'm not some weak wolf shifter like the ones you fought yesterday."

So, he knew what had happened, and he was nervous. The vileness of his soul rolled off him and into me. "Good. They were easy." Needing to intimidate him as much as possible, I charged first and punched his jaw.

His neck snapped back, and his eyes widened with rage. "Fine. Let's do this." He lunged toward me, using his weight as his weapon.

Good, that was what I wanted him to do. That was what all men did—tried to use their strength against me. But I was faster and more agile than they were.

I spun out of the way, and the bear ran into the tree I'd

been standing in front of. I twisted around and kicked his back, making his head slam hard into the trunk.

A loud growl shook his body as he pushed off and pivoted toward me. A large cut had opened on his forehead, and the blood dripped down his face and into his eye.

Not bothering with threats, he leaped at me and wrapped his hands around my waist, tipping me over. I landed on my back with his full weight on top of me.

"You won't win against me," he spat as he grabbed my arms, pulling them up on both sides of my head.

Yes. Irrational rage. That was what I wanted.

I forced myself to ignore the pain in my shoulders and kneed him in the balls. His face blanched as agony radiated through his body, and his hold on my wrists slackened.

Tapping into my wolf strength, I rolled him off me and kicked him in the stomach. He groaned as he curled into the fetal position, one hand wrapping around his belly and the other going to his family jewels.

As if he wasn't sure which one needed protecting more.

My biggest problem was that I had a decision to make, and one that I couldn't take lightly. I pulled the knife from my ankle and lifted it as I approached him.

Should I kill him or let him live? He wasn't a great person, but could I kill someone in cold blood?

"Do it!" he yelled. "Kill me."

And that answered my question. He was desperate for death. "No, you're coming with me." But I had no clue how to take him. I didn't have handcuffs or rope. How the hell would I restrain him?

My mind ran over possible scenarios as the guy reached for his belt buckle. My body coiled, ready for another round of fighting. *I'm on the side of the road. I took down a bear shifter who's getting ready to attack again.*

I'll be there shortly, Griffin said. *Just stay alive.*

Easier said than done. I held my knife, ready for battle, but the guy didn't remove his belt—rather, he pulled something out. It looked like a pill.

No! Surely that couldn't be what I thought it was.

I rushed toward him as he put the pill in his mouth.

"What are you doing?" I screamed, as I reached him.

I squeezed his cheeks, trying to make him open his mouth, but he clamped it closed. His eyes widened as his body jerked.

"Spit it out." I smacked his face like that was going to make him listen to me. *"Now."*

His mouth finally opened, but spit bubbled out as he choked. His eyes bulged, and his body convulsed.

Tears dripped down my face as I watched the life fade from his eyes. I didn't know the guy, and he obviously wasn't a nice person, but that didn't mean he had to die. Not like this.

Who the hell was after me? They had to be bad if this guy was willing to kill himself instead of facing their wrath.

CHAPTER TWO

Wings flapped overhead, and I tore my gaze from the dead man. I wiped away my tears and stood, knife in hand.

My mind still felt fuzzy from whatever drug remained in my system, so being able to fight as well as I had was a godsend. My breathing became labored as I scanned the area, waiting for whoever was coming to appear.

At least, the adrenaline was helping ward off the fogginess threatening to overtake me again.

With my luck, it'd be that damn crow that got away yesterday from the battle scene. He must have reported straight to their leader in order for them to have sent more people to capture me so quickly.

As the flapping grew louder, my body tensed. Whoever was coming wasn't trying to be quiet. Instead, they were announcing their arrival.

When a familiar rose scent wafted toward me, my heart started beating once more.

Rosemary.

As if she'd heard her name, the dark angel flew between

the two large trees and landed several feet away. Her long, straight mahogany hair was pulled into a low ponytail, emphasizing her piercing purple stardust eyes. She wore a black shirt that matched the color of her feathers and contrasted with her fair skin.

Her forehead wrinkled as she took in the scene.

I blinked a few times, trying to wrap my head around the fact that she was here. "How did you find me so quickly?"

"I've been flying around ever since I was alerted that someone had kidnapped you." Rosemary pulled in her wings, which then disappeared into her back. "I was about to turn around to head north when I heard squealing tires. I thought I'd better check it out."

"Well, I'm glad you did." I ran my fingers through my tangled hair. "Luckily, he was alone, or I might not have gotten the upper hand."

She strolled to the bear and squatted next to him. "He killed himself?" she asked in surprise.

"Yeah, he did." I was still reeling over that fact, too. "I took him down, and he went for his belt. I thought he was getting ready to fight again, but he took a pill."

"I swear, things have gotten even more interesting since you showed up." Rosemary stood. "We need to get out of here before someone finds us."

"Yeah, but how?" If a human pulled up right now, we would have a huge problem—but it wasn't like I had a shovel handy. "There's no way we can hide the car and him." It was daylight, so anyone driving by would be able to see us from the road. "But we need to check the car out before we leave. He might have left something important in it."

"Fine. See if you can find anything incriminating. I'll

deal with the bear." She bent down and picked up the huge man all by herself.

"What are you going to do with him?" I got that we needed to divide and conquer, but that bear was huge—and dead weight, now.

Her wings appeared behind her once again. "I'll figure something out." She took off, flying low and using the trees as cover.

I watched her disappear—gaping and shocked at her show of strength—before reality snapped back around me.

There was no time to stand here idly.

The driver's door remained open, and the engine was still running. The bear had been so focused on reaching me that I was almost surprised to find he'd put the car in park.

Rosemary found me. I linked with Griffin as I surveyed the tan interior of the sedan. The car looked to be several years old, but in good condition. I ripped off a piece of my shirt, using it to avoid leaving fingerprints, and leaned over to pop the glove box.

Where is she? Griffin asked. *Are you hurt?*

No, but the bear shifter who kidnapped me killed himself. I filled Griffin in on everything as I searched the car. There was no registration, which didn't surprise me. They could've stolen the car, for all I knew.

A shrill ringtone came from the backseat, and I glanced over my shoulder and saw a phone. I reached over the seat and grabbed it, but before I could answer, the ringing stopped.

This had to be a burner phone, which would come in handy. Maybe when things settled down, we could call the person who was trying to capture me. At least I hadn't come up empty-handed.

Rosemary stepped from the trees again. She hurried to

me, alarm etched on her face. "A few cars will be passing by soon—we need to go. Otherwise, you'll have a ton of questions to answer." She stretched her arms over her head. "Unfortunately, I can't carry you after dealing with that bear. We're going to have to take it by foot."

"No worries." I appreciated that she'd handled him by herself. She'd managed to do it faster than if I'd tried to help. And she was right, we had to move. But unfortunately, I couldn't shift into my animal, which would make everything take longer. There were already enough people who knew that I was a silver wolf; I didn't need to add more to the equation. And I didn't want to take the possibly stolen car, so, walking it was.

"Well, come on." She grabbed my arm and pulled me toward the tree line.

We walked in silence until we were deep enough into the woods that no one could see us from the road. I kept an eye out anyway, thankful that the trees and bushes were in full bloom. I was moving slower than I liked, still impacted by the drug they'd given me. At some point, this stuff would have to wear off. It didn't help my paranoia that there was a tickle in the back of my mind, hinting that I was forgetting something important.

After a few minutes of silence, Rosemary said, "Tell Griffin that we'll be at Shadow Lake shortly. We're about five miles away. He can pick you up there."

Being told what to do rubbed me the wrong way, but I pushed my annoyance down; she'd come and helped me when no one else had been able to find me. I followed her instructions—alerting Griffin to the plan—then paused, trying to determine the best course of action.

"Why are you here?" I finally asked, rather bluntly. The

few times I'd been direct with her, she seemed to appreciate the straightforwardness, so I'd go with that.

"Let's see." Rosemary pursed her lips. "A girl went missing on Shadow Ridge University's campus in broad daylight."

"A wolf." If she thought just telling me facts that I already knew would halt my line of questioning, she would soon learn otherwise. "Not an angel."

"What?" She gasped and placed a hand on her chest. "You've got to be kidding me."

"Seriously." I wasn't in the mood for witty banter. "This is the third time you've helped me, and I have no clue why." When someone had spray-painted a silver wolf on the brick wall outside my place of employment in an attempt—a successful one, I was still annoyed to admit—to draw me out, she'd gone back to Shadow City to figure out who knew about me. She'd helped us fight the attackers yesterday and had healed Griffin from a near-fatal gunshot wound, and today she'd helped me with the bear shifter and was now escorting me to my mate.

"Maybe I want to stay on your mate's good side." Rosemary kept her gaze forward, not meeting my eyes.

"Bullshit." I was done playing games. "You insult him at every opportunity, and you don't seem impressed with wolves, in general. What do you get out of helping me?"

She chuckled, her irises lightening in the sunlight. "You're right. I think Griffin is a tool. He's caused a lot of problems for Shadow City because of his reluctance to take his father's place."

"Among the wolves?" Apparently, there were random attacks on wolves pretty consistently. I had been the target of one such attack at Dick Harding's bar.

"No, not just the wolves." Rosemary inhaled sharply.

"There's an order to the city. Each race has a handful of representatives, but the city itself has an overall leader. Griffin is supposed to be that leader but has refused to step up, and it's caused discord among all the supernaturals. It's just been messy."

"Which brings me back to my question." I arched an eyebrow.

"There are a few reasons." She wrinkled her nose. "And at this point, I don't want to explain them to you."

"Then why should I trust you?" That was the real question I needed answered. I didn't sense bad vibes from her, but I didn't necessarily get warm fuzzy ones, either. She was strong, which I respected, but I needed to understand where her loyalties lie.

"I know one of your secrets, so I guess it's fair that you know one of mine." She stopped and faced me. "But this stays between us, do you understand?"

"Of course."

"I grew up believing that the silver wolves were dead." She nibbled on her bottom lip. "But Mom would tell me stories of the past and about this special race of wolves."

"You grew up hearing stories about us?" That was a little surreal.

"Yes, and each story centered on the fact that silver wolves were special. And that if they were still alive, we would be doing anything we could to protect them like we should have done before." She shrugged. "So I figure, if Mom believes that angels should have helped the silver wolves, then there has to be something to it."

"So, you told her about me?"

"No, I did not." She shook her head and picked up the pace. "There's enough going on with the angel members of the council—I didn't want to add your secret to it. Mom already has her plate full. Right now, only the handful of us know, and it should stay that way."

I was okay with that. The fewer people who knew about me, the easier it would be to determine who might be working against me. "Well, thank you."

"You're welcome." She gestured to the right. "The lake is there."

Lapping water affirmed what she said, and I scanned the murky lake water, looking for any signs of people out here besides us.

The rest of the trek was made in silence, and soon, a familiar Navigator came into view.

My heart rate increased as my legs took on a life of their own. The connection between us *tugged*, and Griffin climbed out of the car, staring straight at me.

My breath caught as his hazel eyes met mine, glowing with his surging wolf. His sculpted face held a strained expression, and his honey-brown hair looked completely disheveled. He rushed toward me and caught me, lifting me up against his six-and-a-half-foot frame. He pulled me into his arms as his scent of myrrh and leather comforted me. His scruff brushed my face as he kissed me. *Thank God, you're okay. I was so damn worried.*

I eagerly responded to his kiss, trying to calm him down. *I'm fine. We're back together now.*

Rosemary cleared her throat. "You two aren't alone."

"Clearly," Griffin grumbled as he pulled away. He ran his fingers down my cheek and checked me over for injuries. "Thank you for finding her."

"No problem. Now, we need to figure out our next steps." Rosemary's jaw twitched.

"What do you mean?" Griffin wrapped an arm around my waist. "I'm taking her home where she belongs."

Rosemary huffed. "She was just attacked there yesterday. She's not safe there, or at work."

"I'll get more guards." Griffin puffed out his chest.

Rosemary lifted a hand. "Oh, because that went *so* well yesterday."

Great, they were already arguing, and it hadn't even been a minute. "She's right." I faced him and touched his shoulder. "Going back to your or Killian's house isn't the best idea. They know where I'm staying, and they have a lot of manpower."

"Then we'll go to the alpha house in Shadow City." Griffin intertwined our fingers. "That's the safest place you could be."

"Not while we don't know who's behind all the attempts to capture me. It could be someone inside the city." We had no clue who we were up against. "Before we alert anyone else that a silver wolf is alive, we need to figure out who's hunting me." A chill ran down my spine.

I truly was being hunted.

"She's right." Rosemary nodded. "I know for a fact that Azbogah and his angel backers wouldn't be thrilled about her existence. We need to focus on one problem at a time instead of having everything come to a head."

Her words resonated with me. "We need to go where this whole thing started." My heart sank, but there was no getting around the truth.

"What do you mean?" Rosemary arched an eyebrow.

"My pack was...*slaughtered.*" My voice broke, but I managed to keep it at least somewhat together. "That's how I ended up in Shadow Ridge, to begin with. My pack home is where we need to start."

"Are you sure about that?" Griffin cupped my face, ignoring the dark angel beside us. "I'll station fifty guards in front of our door at all times if that's what it'll take to keep you safe."

"But that's the thing." His concern warmed my heart. So much had changed between us in a short amount of time. "I wouldn't be truly safe. I'd be more of a prisoner." I refused to live like that, which meant I had to face my biggest fear. "For our future, I need to go back to the pack neighborhood right outside of Chattanooga and see if anything was left behind. The answers may be in the past."

My stomach revolted the entire way to my family home. Rosemary was going to meet us there later after checking in with her family, and Killian would be there a few minutes after us.

The memories of that day were crisp and clear. The sound of the guns firing, all of the dead bleeding out on the ground, and my own father being attacked while I slipped away to safety; nightmares that still haunted me whether I was asleep or awake. For the past month, with all the death and heartache that had come my way, a reaper might have been following me around. I'd heard that there were a few that got involved when life became unbalanced, but there hadn't been any signs, so that wasn't plausible.

"Are you sure about this?" Griffin's hand tightened on mine. "We don't have to go back there, or I could at least have some people go first and check everything out."

"No. I bet they gave up on me coming back, but we'll be careful, just in case." Hell, I'd never expected to willingly go back. "And the more people we alert to the plan, the more likely the wrong person will find out. If we want to see if something was left behind, going now is our best bet."

Griffin took the all-too-familiar turn that bent around a section of woods leading into the pack neighborhood. The bright sun sparkled in a cloudless sky, almost as if the past few days had all been just a nightmare. But the pain that gripped me as I prepared to see the death and destruction I'd left behind reminded me that it was, in fact, reality.

When the neighborhood came into view, I sucked in a breath...and couldn't believe my eyes.

CHAPTER THREE

"I ... I don't understand." My brain was still fuzzy, but that wasn't the problem. I scanned the road leading into the pack neighborhood—there wasn't a body in sight. From what I could see, each modest brick house looked untouched, as if the slaughter had been only a dream.

The image of that day blurred with today, and I shook my head, trying to keep a hold on reality.

Griffin clutched the steering wheel, his knuckles turning white as he slowed the car just outside the pack neighborhood. "What's wrong?"

I bit the inside of my cheek so I wouldn't laugh. The question wasn't funny, but I was teetering on the edge of insanity, which unsettled me. "That day...there were so many bodies." They'd littered the ground every ten feet, if that. "Where did they all go?"

"Do you think there could be survivors?" Griffin pulled over to the side of the road under the shade of several large oak trees grouped together at the edge of the woods and stopped the car. "Maybe they were able to fight back after you left."

His words gave me foolish hope that I had to squash down. "No. I don't feel any pack connections. If there were survivors, I would know." I got out of the vehicle, leaving the door open. A cool spring breeze stirred around me, carrying the familiar scents of magnolias and redbuds of my home.

"Should we head back?" Griffin asked.

"No, going back to Shadow Ridge won't be safe." We'd already had that conversation, but I understood his instinct to go somewhere he knew. "This is the safest place to be." At least, for the moment.

"Okay." He sighed. "Let's check things out while we wait on Killian."

"How long until he gets here?"

He pulled his phone from his pocket and glanced at the text. "Probably ten to fifteen minutes."

That would give us enough time to run around and make sure there weren't any surprises before pulling Griffin's Navigator into the neighborhood, alerting watchful eyes. "Sounds like a plan."

"I'll let him know what we're doing in case he gets here before we get back." He turned off the car and shot off a text before getting out.

As I waited on him, I inhaled and exhaled slowly, focusing on calming breaths to keep my racing heart from exploding. I didn't want to be here. In fact, this was the last place in the world I wanted to be. I'd figured seeing my pack's home would be hard, but it was so much more than that. Everywhere I looked, memories of my childhood replayed in my mind.

We'd used the large circular grassy knoll for our training sessions that dad led, and the faint laughter of playing chase in the woods tickled my ears.

This safe haven had been turned into a place of anger,

hatred, and so much remorse. What I wouldn't give to run in the woods with Zoe again, or for my dad to yell at me for flinching and giving away my next move. Or to experience, again, how Mom always listened when I felt like Dad—or anyone else—was being unfair, guiding me into considering the other person's viewpoint, which had molded me into the person I was today.

"Hey," Griffin rasped, as he pulled me into his arms. "We can find a hotel room or something. We don't have to stay here."

"That would put us around people and other shifters, which could make it easier for them to locate us." I appreciated what he was trying to do, but this was where we needed to be. I could feel it, even if I didn't like it.

I kissed him, using our bond for comfort. I needed him in order to get through the next little bit. "Let's scout around before Killian gets here." I faced the neighborhood. *Why don't you go right and I'll take the left?*

You want us to split up? Griffin sounded less than thrilled. *I figured we'd go together.*

If we find something—or someone—it'll be better if they think we're alone. I didn't want something to happen to both of us. *That way we'll have the element of surprise.*

Do you not realize what I went through when you disappeared? What we all went through? he linked as his fingers tangled in my hair, making my body warm. *I went insane looking for you. I don't think I can go through something like that again.*

My fingers trailed over his chin, his scruff biting the tips. I couldn't imagine how it had felt, and I hated that he'd gone through that. *I understand, but this is for the best. You won't be far, and we'll be linked the entire time.*

Fine, but if there is any sort of sign that we aren't alone, you let me know immediately. Griffin stared into my eyes. *I get that you're trained to fight and I'm not, but you're my mate. I need to know that you'll let me protect you, if it comes to that.*

We're a team. I stared into his eyes and pushed my emotions hard toward him so he could feel my sincerity. We'd had a rocky start with me pretending to be Killian's girlfriend and both of us trying to fight our connection. But we were finally here and on the same page, and we had to start trusting one another. *If even one thing seems out of sorts, I'll let you know. Also, we should stay in human form so we can talk with Killian when he gets here.*

He must have seen whatever he was looking for in my eyes because he nodded. *All right. Let's get this over with.*

I pecked him one last time and took off toward the tree line on the left.

His footsteps grew farther away as he followed my lead, heading in the opposite direction.

The neighborhood is one huge circle. I ran into the trees, trying to push away the memories that hung at the forefront of my mind. *We'll meet up on the other side.*

Got it, he responded.

Silence descended as I ran through trees that I knew like the back of my hand. Woodland animals fluttered and rustled around me like they hadn't a care in the world, which seemed unjustly cruel. Life had moved on. It shouldn't have been possible.

It wasn't fair.

The stain of my pack's murder should have had some sort of impact on the world.

Each silver wolf who'd died had vowed to protect the entire supernatural world—not just the wolves—so their loss should've been mourned by everyone. And yet, it was as if they had never existed.

It was as if the silver wolves had been erased from history. Atticus had known about us, but he hadn't shared the information with Griffin. So...who else knew?

Something wasn't adding up, and unfortunately, neither Griffin's dad nor my own were here to answer questions.

I tapped into my wolf, trying to keep my emotions in check. I ran a little faster than normal, afraid that if I slowed, the memories would catch up to me and crash all around.

However, when I turned toward the alpha's home—*my* home—there was no saving me.

Even though it wasn't possible, I was back in time, reliving that horrible day.

Dad stood in the center of the yard, grimacing as he clutched his side. Blood stained his white shirt, and his silver eyes—so similar to my own—stared at me. I could hear his voice clearly. "You need to go *now*." His irises had darkened to steel, and his silver hair had become a tarnished gray. The handsome alpha I grew up knowing had looked so damn old.

"Daddy?" I whispered, rushing toward the mirage. A part of me knew that he wasn't here—that it was a figment of my imagination—but I couldn't see past it. All I wanted to do was hug at least one of my parents, at least one person I missed more than life itself, and have him tell me everything would be okay.

But when I reached him and tried to hug him, all I touched was air.

His image vanished right before my eyes, and the overwhelming sense of loss coursed through me again.

I didn't know what to do or how to proceed. How I

wished I could go back in time and cherish our moments together. I'd thought I still had so much time left with him—that he'd be here to teach me so much more—but I'd been so damn wrong. Instead of being annoyed with every new lesson for the day, I should've worked harder.

When he'd told me I needed to push through, I should've listened.

At the end of the day, he and Mom were the two people who always made me feel safe, and those gunmen had taken them away from not only me, but the entire world.

They couldn't get away with that. I refused to let the pack's sacrifice be in vain. If there was one thing I could do right by for all of my pack, it would be to become the very person Dad had hoped for, and the alpha Mom had known I could be.

A kickass alpha who every man would submit to.

Babe? Griffin linked. *Did you find something?*

The concern in his voice forced me to center. I sucked in a breath, trying to push back the raging emotions inside. I needed to calm down. *I'm fine. I'm sorry.*

Why are you sorry? he asked, almost frantically. *Did something happen?*

I could hear his footsteps now, rushing toward me. There was no telling how long I'd been standing here. *I... I just...* My inner voice cracked, and his concern wafted through our bond.

No matter how hard I tried to center myself, it was like I couldn't stay above water. My emotions flowed underneath, trying to drown me. *I'm home and...*

Griffin stepped into the yard and raced toward me. He pulled me into his arms, holding me tight as he pressed his face to the top of my head. *I'm here,* he whispered. *You're not alone.*

Tears fell like a waterfall as I mourned the deaths of my parents and pack. I'd thought I had grieved for them, but I'd been wrong. I'd been pushing it off to stay in survival mode. Focusing on the threat and surviving day to day. But being here and having to face what had happened... their deaths were catching up.

But Griffin's words stuck with me.

I wasn't alone.

Somehow, in this harsh new reality, I'd found not only my fated mate, but a brother, too. And even though neither one of them could replace my pack or parents, they were so damn important. With them by my side, I would be able to continue on and become the daughter my parents always wanted me to be.

Returning Griffin's embrace, I filled my nose with his comforting scent. There was no place I'd rather be than in his arms. *It just kind of snuck up on me.*

I know that feeling all too well. Griffin leaned back and smiled sadly. *So, this was your home?*

Yeah. I steadied myself, almost expecting to see the broken memory of Dad again—but this time, when I looked at the house, the backyard remained empty of ghosts.

But not the memories.

I turned to the red and yellow hibiscus and purple hydrangeas that lined the entrance to my house. "Mom and I planted those flowers last year, and we were so excited to see them bloom." Yet another thing she and I wouldn't ever do together.

Tears threatened my eyes, so I turned toward the woods. The healthy green leaves of ash, oak, and maple trees contrasted with the death I now associated with this place.

The sound of Killian's truck alerted me to his presence.

"We better go meet him before he gets concerned." I

scanned the area, looking for any sort of sign that we might not be alone. Nothing stirred.

The two of us took off back toward the Navigator, quickly running the two miles to the vehicle. When we reached the Navigator, we found Killian leaning against his black truck, which he'd parked behind Griffin's SUV.

His warm, dark-chocolate eyes lit up when he saw me, and he pushed off his truck and hurried in my direction. His cappuccino-brown hair hung in his face, and with each step he took, it flopped to the side. He hugged me tight against his athletic body, and his musky sandalwood scent helped calm a part of my soul.

"Don't ever scare us like that again," Killian growled.

"Hey, it wasn't her fault," a familiar female said as she climbed down from the truck.

My body tensed as I stared at Sierra. Her sandy-blonde hair was pulled into a ponytail, and her gray eyes scanned me. She was a few inches shorter than me, but her big personality compensated for it.

"Wait...I thought you were alone." I didn't like the fact that Killian had brought someone with him. I got that Sierra had been his late sister's best friend, but the fewer people who knew about me and my pack, the safer we all would be. I scowled at Griffin, wondering why he hadn't told me this little fact.

"Hey, I didn't know." He lifted both hands. "When I tore out of the coffee shop, Killian was alone."

"I'm sorry. I didn't mean to intrude, but when I heard about you being taken, I told Killian I wanted to help." Sierra put her hands in her pockets. "There have been so many attacks. The other day, my sister got injured in one of the outbreaks, and Killian told me about your pack being killed." She paused as her jaw clenched. "It's got to stop. The unrest is spreading farther and farther."

"I promise she's trustworthy—and worst case, I can command her not to share." Killian placed a hand on his heart. "I wouldn't have brought her here if I doubted she was trustworthy."

"Okay." It wasn't like I'd planned on shifting to my animal form anyway. I needed to stay human as much as possible so there weren't any other accidental sightings.

"Besides, I thought you might need a friend who doesn't have a penis." She pointed at Griffin and Killian. "Because even though they try to be good guys, they're kinda assholes."

I laughed, surprising myself. "We all have our moments." Maybe it wasn't a bad thing for her to be here. If she could make me laugh like that, she could be a godsend.

"True that." She lifted a hand, but there was sadness in her eyes. "So what's the plan?"

That was the real question. "We need to find clues. Anything that might lead us to whoever killed my pack and attacked me in Shadow Ridge. The problem is someone came here and cleaned up the bodies."

"Which means they were making sure they didn't leave anything behind." Killian pursed his lips. "That means it's someone organized."

"Yes, but we already knew that," Griffin sighed, "between the attack outside our houses and them taking her from the coffee shop."

We could stand out here and speculate all day. "Our best bet is to look for answers. They have to be here somewhere." I hated to suggest it, but the first place to look would be the last place I wanted to go. "Let's start at my house. After all, my father was the alpha, and he had a study. A few days before we were attacked, he was going in there and locking the door a lot." I couldn't believe that it had taken me until now to remember that little fact.

"I agree." Sierra waved to the vehicles. "That's the place to start. Let's go."

We got into the vehicles and Killian followed Griffin to the house. As we drove past the neighborhood houses, my pain somehow increased. And the closer we got to my house, the more hurt coursed through me. I didn't know what kind of state I'd be when we arrived back at home.

House after house looked untouched. The only sign that no one was around was the overgrown grass that now covered the yards. Soon, the turn to the back of the neighborhood and my house appeared. I felt as if I couldn't breathe again when we pulled into my driveway and got out.

I made my way to the side of the house where the air conditioner unit sat. I bent and picked up the key that was hidden under the rocks surrounding the unit. As I straightened, a branch snapped not ten feet away.

CHAPTER FOUR

I spun around, searching for the source of the noise. My heart pounded so hard my ears rang, and I sniffed, searching for any scents outside the norm.

Nothing.

Needing to make sure, I slowly walked to the tree line... and a faint scent of musk tickled my nose. However, it wasn't strong enough for someone to have been there moments ago. This scent was a few days old, probably from whoever had cleaned up the pack neighborhood. A squirrel or something must have run by and caused the disturbance.

Is something wrong? Griffin asked as he made his way toward me, following my gaze into the woods.

That was a tricky question, even though he hadn't meant for it to be. *I heard a branch snap, but it must have been an animal.* I forced myself to turn back to the house that I dreaded entering. I was tempted to say we needed to scout out the area more, but that would only prolong the inevitable. Searching the house was the best bet for finding clues or, at least, something that could point us in the right direction.

Putting one foot in front of the other, I made it to the sturdy, red chestnut door of my childhood home, but the door was already slightly ajar. I pushed the door open the rest of the way, trying not to freeze. If I paused, there was no telling when I'd finally get going again.

The living room looked the same as it had that morning when I'd left to walk to the river. The beige, cloth couch sat against the tan wall with Dad's brown, leather recliner in the corner. The news flickered on the television with the sound muted, and the remote control sat on the arm of the recliner. That was where Dad always sat.

Sadness tugged on my heart, but I pushed it away. If I started crying now, I wasn't sure if I'd ever stop.

I entered the house, stepping onto the dark walnut floor. The scent of lavender—Mom's favorite fragrance—overwhelmed me.

My throat went dry as I held back the tears burning my eyes. I didn't want to break down in front of everyone.

I had to be strong.

Sierra stepped beside me. "This is kind of creepy."

That was one way of putting it. "It feels like they should be somewhere in the house." I tried to keep the emotion from my voice, but it leaked through, so I pushed forward through the room and toward the hallway.

The three of them followed me, and I paused at the large eat-in kitchen on the right. All of the maple cabinets were closed—which was the norm—but the large empty pot on the black stove and a sink full of washed-off dishes made it clear that something was wrong. Mom hated a cluttered kitchen and always told me that the trick was cleaning as you cooked.

Just another reminder that they were truly gone.

"What time of day did they attack?" Griffin asked as he took my hand.

"Midday on the new moon." I noted that two of the chairs at the round table were pulled out; probably due to Mom and Dad sitting down with their coffee. *When we are at our weakest,* I linked with Griffin. I got that Killian trusted Sierra, but I didn't yet. Trust had to be earned at this point.

"New moon?" Sierra parroted. "I guess that's one way of remembering the date."

I wasn't going to touch that comment. Anything I could've added would have exposed me further.

Killian cleared his throat. "So, where should we begin looking?"

"Why don't you and Sierra search the woods and see if they left something behind or, at least, find what they did with the de—" I couldn't finish the sentence. I wanted to know where the pack was buried...or if they even were.

Sierra grimaced. "Yes, we can do that."

She understood my meaning, which relieved me. I didn't have to say it after all.

Needing to change the direction of the conversation, I said, "Griffin and I can search here." I wanted to be the one who went through Dad's stuff—there was no telling what I might find.

"Are you sure?" Killian asked. "We can help—"

"No, I need to do this." I had to. Depending on what I found, I might need to process it a little while on my own.

"You heard her." Griffin stood behind me, placing his hands on my shoulders. "If you guys need anything, we're only a phone call away."

"That sounds like a plan." Sierra saluted. "We can circle

deeper in the woods and see what we find. They had to leave something behind."

"Let's hope so." I needed answers.

The two of them headed to the door as Killian called out, "We'll be back soon."

When the front door closed again, I spun around, placing my head on Griffin's shoulder. I needed a moment to brace myself for what came next. It was hard enough being in the house, but going into Dad's study and my parents' room would make things even worse.

I'll be right here with you the entire way. Griffin pressed a kiss to my forehead. *We can take as long as you need.*

But the longer I put it off, the harder this would be. *No, let's get moving before Sierra gets back.* I headed back down the hallway, straight to my room on the left. I wanted to look in there and make sure nothing had been left behind by the hunters.

Going through my own room shouldn't be as hard as the others, so it made sense to start there.

I stepped inside, and the scent of unfamiliar shifters hit my nose. I hadn't smelled anyone until this room, which meant they'd spent a lot of time in it. The silver walls of my room felt as though they were mocking me—like I'd tempted fate by matching them to my hair.

The collage of me and the pack was missing, and the teal sheets of my bed were crumpled. Mom had been a drill sergeant when it came to cleanliness, so it was another sign that people had gone through the house.

"'This is your room?" Griffin asked, as he stepped in behind me.

"Yeah. It was." It didn't feel like home anymore. There were too many horrible memories for that...at least, for now.

"Our pack has lived in this town ever since we left Shadow City."

"Why did the silver wolves leave Shadow City?" Griffin asked as he walked to my small bookshelf, scanning the titles of the classics that I loved to read.

"Honestly, I'm not sure." Dad and I had assumed we had so much more time for him to teach me things. "I know we were in danger there, but I have no clue why, or from who."

"It's strange that my dad knew that you existed." Griffin slowly turned, taking in the room. "He never told me about you all, either, but your dad did come and visit. I vaguely remember him."

I walked to my closet and looked through my clothes. Nothing seemed to be missing, except for my pictures, which made sense. They'd probably taken them back to wherever they were based to get additional resources looking for me. "I think we're good here. Let's go look at Dad's study. I'm assuming that's where they did most of their searching."

He followed me into the study, and I took in the scattered papers on Dad's huge mahogany desk. "This was the third bedroom. He converted it into his office." I flipped through the papers, finding bills and other records, but nothing substantial. Yet, I knew he hid stuff somewhere.

Griffin walked to the filing cabinets that lined the wall. "I guess I'll start here, and you search his desk?"

I didn't have a better suggestion. "Sure." I opened the top drawer of the desk, expecting to find the cabinet keys, but instead, I found it bare. Yet another sign that someone had searched the house.

However, Griffin was able to open the cabinet drawers without any problems. Whoever searched it hadn't taken the time to lock it and put the keys back. Either they didn't care if someone figured out that they'd been here, or they thought no one would show up and realize what had happened—beyond someone from the electric or water company looking to get paid or turn off the water.

Either way, we had a lot to dig through. I sat in my dad's chair as a heaviness seemed to press on my shoulders.

My entire life, I'd known that I would be sitting at my father's desk one day, but I could never have imagined it like this. He'd been taken from me far too soon, and I didn't know how to recover. A piece of me had died that day—along with him and the others—but I refused to cower. Whoever was after me wanted to break me and have me as his own, personal breeder. But what he didn't know was that silver wolves reproduced slower than normal wolves. Dad had explained that our slowness to reproduce was due to our stronger powers—that nature had a way of balancing power so that it didn't swing in favor of one race alone.

That didn't matter. The man hunting me didn't give a damn about the logistics. He wanted control, or at least the illusion of it.

So, I did the only thing I knew to do.

I rolled up my sleeves and began digging.

THE ENTIRE DAY had been one emotional ride.

The four of us sat around my kitchen table in silence. Killian had run out to get some all-meat pizzas, so I choked down a slice—only because both Griffin and Killian kept watching me. But the food sat uncomfortably in my stomach.

"Are you sure you're good staying here tonight?" Griffin asked, for the fifth time.

"It's the safest place for us." And it would keep us close to Dad's study so we could continue our search in the morning. "I have everything I need here." Except for my pack.

Killian and Sierra hadn't found much in the woods. They'd searched about half the neighborhood's perimeter before calling it a day and going to grab the food for dinner.

If I hadn't known better, I would've thought I got run over by a train. I felt incredibly hungover—probably from the drugs—plus, my emotional well-being was subpar. Every so often, I thought I heard Dad's footsteps coming down the hall, and the realization that I would never hear that again slammed into me.

"Since that's settled, let's get you to bed." Griffin's face creased with concern. "You've had one hell of a day."

Bed did sound nice. I stood and glanced at Sierra and Killian. "Let me get you two some sheets for the couch and recliner."

"Nope, we're good. I saw some blankets in the hall closet." Sierra waved me off. "You go get some rest. I'll take care of it."

I sort of wanted to argue but just didn't have it in me. "If you do need something, just let me know."

"Will do," Sierra said as she pointed at Griffin. "Now go get your mate in bed."

"Yes, ma'am." He chuckled and took my hand.

When the two of us entered my room, I climbed into bed, not even worrying about changing clothes. My body seemed to weigh a ton, and the thought of standing any longer didn't hold any appeal.

Griffin lay down next to me and pulled me into his arms. His fingertips brushed my arm, making me sigh. I rolled toward him and stared into his eyes.

I'd never get tired of looking at him, and I wasn't sure

what would've happened if he wasn't here with me. A part of me knew that I wouldn't have been nearly as strong.

He kissed me gently, parting my lips with his tongue.

I responded to his kiss in earnest, needing to feel him.

Hey, you need your rest. He pulled back a little. *You almost passed out while eating.*

I did need my rest, but I also needed him to help me feel alive. *I want you to make me forget this shitty day.* I kissed him eagerly, making my intentions clear. *I need you.*

Why don't you take a nap first? he growled, trying to remain strong.

My hand unbuttoned his jeans as I deepened our kiss. *No.* I slipped my hand inside his boxers, stroking him.

Dammit. He groaned as his hands gripped my waist and pulled me on top of him.

I rocked against him, needing to feel the friction. I grabbed the hem of his shirt and yanked it over his head; then, clawed down his chest, enjoying the feel of his skin.

His hands slipped under my shirt and removed it from my body. He reached around me and unfastened my bra, and my breasts fell right into his face. He captured a nipple between his teeth, flicking it with his tongue.

The ache grew deeper inside me as my body warmed. He rolled me off him and stood at the side of the bed. Then he grabbed my jeans and panties and dragged them off my body.

"You're so damn beautiful," he rasped as he kicked off his jeans and boxers. He leaned over me and kissed me to the point that my head grew dizzy.

The scents of our arousal mixed, making the room smell intoxicating. I tried getting up, wanting to take control, but he grabbed my arms and held them at the sides of my head.

We're supposed to be going slow, he chastised me, as his fingers pinched my nipples.

A low moan escaped as my body caught on fire. *This is slow.*

He chuckled, sounding so damn sexy. *No, it's not.*

I wrapped my legs around his waist, enjoying the feel of him rubbing against me.

He groaned huskily, nearly making me come unglued.

Please. I begged, not even embarrassed.

Fine. He placed his hand between us, positioning himself, and thrust into me hard.

Pleasure rocketed through me as he lifted my hips, hitting deeper inside. With his free hand, he rubbed circular motions between my legs, making every cell in my body ignite.

He surrounded my senses; every smell, touch, and taste belonged to him. I opened myself up, wanting him to know everything I felt—between everything that had happened that day, and this moment. The words *I love you* passed through my mind.

His emotions poured into me like a damn breaking. *I love you too,* he linked as orgasms surged through both of us.

We breathed out together and stilled. My body was completely satiated, and finally, a sense of peace settled over me.

Eventually, I stood and put on my pajamas. Griffin followed my lead, and soon, we both crawled back into bed. He cuddled me in his arms, and my eyes closed of their own accord. Within seconds, I began dozing off. My body relaxed, but before sleep completely overtook me, a memory popped into my brain.

I sat straight up in bed and clenched my teeth. "I remember who drugged me."

CHAPTER FIVE

G riffin's eyes glowed brightly in the dark room as his
wolf surged forward. "What do you mean? I thought
the guy who kidnapped you killed himself."

"Well, yes, but he wasn't the one who knocked me out at
the coffee shop." The memory of the familiar footsteps
replayed in my mind, followed by the prick and the apology.
"Carter injected me with something."

"What?" Griffin growled. "When I reached the coffee
shop, trying to find you after you asked for help, he told me
someone took you."

"Because the bear shifter did take me. He was the one
driving the car." The betrayal sat hard on my chest as the
reality of the situation landed on me. I got that Carter and I
only worked together, but I'd thought we were at least somewhat friends—and I hadn't sensed any bad vibes from him.
The next words hurt to say. "He knocked me out for him."

"I'm going to inform Killian, since Carter's part of his
pack, and then kill him." Griffin stood, and a vein popped
between his eyebrows as his body tensed with anger. "I'll rip
him limb from limb, starting with his dick."

Okay, he actually went to the male appendage first, but I had to admit the thought had merit. Even though Killian was Carter's alpha, technically, Griffin ruled over the pack because he was the Shadow City alpha. So, Griffin could yank Carter's dick off without penalty.

I rubbed my arms, trying to fight off the cold sinking into my bones. I was even more exhausted; I'd almost been asleep when the memory woke me. The day had been long and hard—both physically and mentally—but this was something that couldn't be ignored.

"Killian should know." Griffin opened the bedroom door and marched down the hallway toward the living room. Each step rattled the pictures that hung on the walls.

"Dude, what the hell?" Killian asked, alarmed. "Are you trying to wake up the dead?"

"The only thing louder than your walking would be someone playing the drums," Sierra complained. "I was almost asleep."

I realized I better get in there before Griffin does something stupid. I forced myself to get up and hurried into the living room, despite my legs feeling like they weighed a hundred pounds each.

"Sterlyn remembered something about her attackers in the coffee shop," Griffin rasped. "And we've got a huge problem."

I joined them in the living room as Sierra sat up on the couch and blinked, asking, "Sterlyn?"

Yeah...we had to be more careful, or we'd wind up having to tell her everything. "That's my real name."

"Thank God. Dove is atrocious. Sterlyn fits you so much better with your hair and silver-purple eyes." She grinned. "Your parents nailed naming you."

She had no clue how true that statement was.

"'Attackers?'" Killian's brows furrowed. "As in plural?"

"Yeah, I thought there was only one, but when I was dozing off, a memory came back to me." I dreaded telling Killian who it was. He and Carter had some kind of bromance I didn't want to interfere with, but we were working as a team, so they all needed to know.

He scowled at me. "Well, then who attacked you?"

I opened my mouth to respond, but Griffin cut me off, "Carter. Your bestie."

"What?" Killian scoffed and shook his head. "No way. He linked with me and told me that someone took her."

God, how many times was I going to have to hear the same thing? "Because the bear shifter took me. That was the only thing he could say without his lie coming to light. But he injected me with God knows what while I was in the pantry, getting the coffee beans that *he* asked me to get. He even apologized before I completely passed out."

"That doesn't make any sense." Killian pulled his phone from his jeans pocket like he was going to make a call. He set it on the edge of the recliner and grimaced. "Look, I'm not trying to be a dick here—"

"Normally, when someone starts off with a comment like that, they're going to be a dick." Sierra placed her feet on the ground and got upright. "So don't even try to qualify it. Just own your damn statement."

Killian glowered at her. "You aren't helping."

"I didn't know I was supposed to." Sierra crossed her arms as she leaned back on the couch.

"Just say what you want to say." I wanted this conversation over with so I could go back to bed. I was struggling to stand on both feet at this point.

Killian scratched the back of his neck. "Are you sure it was Carter? If you were drugged—"

The question stung. "Do you honestly think I would accuse someone if I wasn't one hundred percent sure?" My feelings were hurt that he was second-guessing me. I got that he'd known Carter longer than me, but I thought we'd developed a bond. Maybe I'd misread the situation.

"Dammit, I didn't mean it like that." Killian ran a hand down his face. "You were drugged, and maybe your memory got distorted. That's all I'm trying to say."

"Dude, if Sterlyn says that he did it, then why are you trying to brush it under the rug?" Griffin wrapped an arm around my waist, glaring at his best friend. "Are you really willing to ignore what she remembers because you don't want to consider the possibility that your pack member hurt her?"

"I don't mean it like that." Killian groaned with frustration. "It's just...Carter and I have been friends since childhood. We grew up in Shadow Ridge together. I know his entire family, and that just doesn't sound like him."

"Maybe he didn't have a choice." Sierra lifted a hand, trying to be the voice of reason. "There's no telling what happened, and I agree with Griffin. Sterlyn is no fool, and if she remembers something, we need to check it out."

My heart warmed from both Griffin and Sierra having my back. Usually, I could count on Killian—but not now. My emotions were raw from the entire day, so I couldn't help but feel vulnerable. Being objective wasn't possible for me right now.

"You're right." Killian's shoulders sagged. "I'm being a dick and not thinking objectively. So, there's only one way to find out, and I want you all to hear what he says to me." Killian swiped his phone.

"No, don't call him." I understood that Killian wanted to confront him, but that wasn't the smart way to handle it. "If you call him and ask, he could disappear. We need to see him in person so we can get a good read and he can't hide, lie, or warn whomever he might be working with. If he is involved, he won't hang around just because you two are friends."

"Then how the hell do we get him here?" Killian threw his hands up. "I can't wiggle my nose and make him appear."

"You do seem kind of witchy." Sierra stuck out her tongue at him. "Especially tonight, so maybe it could work."

Those two really did act like siblings. It was clear that they had grown up together.

"I have Rosemary's number." Griffin paced in the center of the room. "I'll call her and see if she's willing to bring him here."

"Why would she help us?" Sierra arched an eyebrow. "You know she's one of the more difficult angels, seeing as who her parents are."

"Who are her parents?" That could mean so many things.

Griffin exhaled. "They're council members who oppose me. They think I'm not strong enough to be the overall leader of the Shadow City and Shadow Ridge wolves."

"I'm not sure what that even means." They tended to forget that I wasn't raised in Shadow Ridge or Shadow City and didn't know the hierarchy.

"From what I've gathered from my history classes, it's similar to the humans' political structure that you've grown up with." He rubbed his hands together. "Like the House and the Senate. Technically, I'm the Senate, while the other two wolf representatives are in the House. So I can veto anything they bring to the table."

"So, what is Rosemary's family?"

"Her mom and dad are the House of Representatives,

with Azbogah being the Senate. So, he can't get anything passed without at least one of them agreeing, and vice versa. They're kind of at odds and at a standstill. Nothing is getting passed on the angel side of things because they're fighting one another."

"Which means I doubt Rosemary will want to get involved with wolf stuff." Sierra waved a hand. "All it would do is cause more of a divide between the angels if they found out."

Interesting. No wonder she was trying to be discreet about helping us. "She and I have an understanding." I wasn't willing to go into more detail than that. "Besides, she'll be willing to help out because of all the attacks going on. The more wolves who are attacked, the more likely a civil war will start."

"True, and if the council members find out that some of our own people who are supposed to be loyal to the city are working against it, things will escalate across the board." Griffin sighed. "Ever since Dad died, things keep going from bad to worse."

I understood that sentiment all too well. "Look, if Rosemary grabs Carter now, his entire family will know something is up. Why don't you call her and see if she can run by the coffee shop in the morning and pick him up? He won't be able to get out of it that way, especially with everyone around as witnesses if he makes a scene."

Griffin's face fell. "I want to question him tonight."

"I know." I did too, but sometimes you couldn't let your desperate need for answers ruin a sound strategy. "But I'm exhausted, and I could really use some sleep. If we aren't well-rested, then we could miss things when talking to him."

"She's right." Killian yawned, though his irises darkened with concern. He was still struggling with the thought of

Carter hurting me. "Just call the angel and see what she says."

"Fine." Griffin pushed some buttons, and soon, a phone was ringing on the other end.

Rosemary answered on the second ring. "Is everything okay?"

"Of course not," Griffin said, annoyingly. "Why else would I be calling?"

This conversation was already starting off great. *Be nice.*

"You call me and then get rude within seconds." Rosemary scoffed. "Give the phone to Sterlyn. I'm done talking to you."

"Gladly." Griffin held the phone toward me.

Well, all right then. I took it and cleared my throat. "Hey, sorry we're calling so late."

"What's wrong?" Rosemary asked, as a door shut on her end.

"I remembered something about the attack earlier." I wasn't sure why, but I didn't dislike her as the others did. She was blunt and said exactly what was on her mind. Maybe the protector side of me appreciated that, because what she said and how she acted mirrored what I felt from inside her; she tried to do the right thing, even when it was difficult. In a way, she was a warrior like the silver wolves.

She remained silent, waiting for me to continue.

"Carter's the one who drugged me."

"That's why the idiot was freaking out." Rosemary sounded disgusted. "He tried to pretend it was because you'd vanished, but I wasn't buying it. I thought it might've been because Griffin was panicking about you being missing, but this makes more sense."

Just like that, she believed me. "Do you think you could run by the coffee shop in the morning and...grab him?"

"You don't want me to get him now?" Rosemary asked, with surprise.

"They could be watching him." The last thing we needed was for her to alert whoever was hunting me to our location. "So it'll be safer if we wait until morning."

"It'll be easier for me too," Rosemary huffed.

"We have to be careful." Bringing him here was risky. "He can't know where we are. We either need him brought here in a way that he can't figure out our location, or we need to meet you somewhere else. But if we do the latter, he could have backup following him."

"Don't worry. I'll take care of it. He won't have a clue where you are," Rosemary reassured me. "Text me your address, and I'll be there early."

We hung up the phone, and I sent her the address.

Then Griffin and I went back to bed...and I fell fast asleep.

A LOUD BANGING WOKE ME. My eyes popped open, and I sat upright, trying to remember where the hell I was. It took a second for me to realize that I was actually in my room back home.

"What the hell?" Griffin grumbled as he stood, and almost tripped over his feet.

"I don't know." I glanced at the clock. It was barely after eight in the morning.

Carter's voice sounded high-pitched. "Where are we? Why did you kidnap me? I need to get back to work."

"Shut up," Rosemary grumbled. "Before I make you."

"You can't just take someone without their permission,"

he said wildly. "Wait until your parents find out what you did!"

That was wild, coming from him. Granted, he had no clue what he was walking into.

"They aren't going to know," Rosemary bit back, as she pounded on the door again. "Because you aren't going to tell them."

We needed to get out there before Rosemary killed him; I needed answers before she slit his throat.

Rosemary opened the front door as Griffin and I joined Sierra and Killian in the living room. Carter's shaggy brown hair was a knotted mess, and his moss-green eyes almost bulged from his face when he saw the four of us standing there. He spun around, rushing past Rosemary to try to get away.

Rosemary grabbed the back of his shirt and yanked him into the house. He stumbled backward, tripping and falling on his ass in front of everyone. As he stared up at us from the ground, he looked more like a child than a twenty-year-old man.

"Uh... Why did you bring me here?" he asked Rosemary, as she shut the door and twisted the lock.

"You know why," she said as she rolled her shoulders and looked at me. "And you owe me. I had to fly his ass here to make sure we weren't followed, and he screamed the whole way."

"Wolves aren't meant to fly," Carter yelled. "They are meant to have their feet on the ground. It's unnatural, what you did to me."

"I'll show you unnatural if you don't shut the fuck up," she sneered.

"Come on, man." Killian held his hand out. "Calm down. There's no reason to freak out."

"Yeah, okay." Carter's arm shook as he took Killian's outstretched hand to stand up.

But his initial reaction proved that my memory was sound. Which meant I had to get a confession from him before he somehow manipulated Killian into believing whatever his story was. That was one thing that I loved about Killian—he was as loyal as they came...but that was also his weakness.

"Yeah, there is." I shifted my weight and placed a hand on my hip. "Because I want to know why you drugged me and handed me off to a bear shifter."

Carter's mouth dropped open, and he took in a shaky breath. "What? No, I didn't."

The sulfuric scent of a lie wafted in the room, confirming what everyone except Killian had already known.

Killian's face twisted into an expression of disappointment, and he closed his eyes.

"You son of a bitch," Griffin yelled, as he punched Carter in the jaw.

CHAPTER SIX

The impact of Griffin's knuckles on Carter's jaw was practically ear-splitting.

Carter's head snapped back and he stumbled, trying to get out of reach. He grabbed his jaw and winced with pain. "What the hell?"

"That's what you have to say for yourself?" Killian's jaw twitched as his nostrils flared. "'What the hell' is all you have to say?" He rushed over to Carter and punched his friend in the gut.

"Ugh." Carter leaned forward, wrapping one arm around his waist as his other hand continued to rub his chin. "Just stop," he groaned.

"Oh, well... Since you asked." Rosemary rolled her eyes. "You're more moronic than I thought."

To prevent them from continuing the beating, I stepped between the two guys and Carter. I scowled at the person who I'd thought was at least sort of my friend. "You've got one second to spill or I'll let Griffin and Killian continue."

Carter tried to straighten up, but he winced, stopping

before he reached his full height. "Look, it was nothing personal," he rasped.

"Dear God." Sierra barked out a laugh and sat on the couch like she was ready to watch a show. "I never thought I'd see the day where I agreed with Rosemary, but hell has officially frozen over. He really is an idiot."

Carter frowned. "Hey! My family is at risk."

"We're well aware," Rosemary said with disdain.

I pushed aside my natural inclination to beat him to a bloody pulp. Acting on emotion would work to our disadvantage, and we already didn't know who we were up against. We didn't need to stack the odds even more in their favor. "Nothing personal is getting the wrong type of cake, or taking a longer lunch break than you were supposed to. Drugging me and passing me off to someone who put me in the trunk of a car is the *definition* of personal."

"I didn't know he was putting you in the trunk!" He at least had the sense to cringe and avert his gaze to the floor.

For him to act so flippant irritated me even more. Who the hell did he think he was? Maybe he was clueless, and we could learn nothing from him.

"Obviously, that makes the entire situation better." Rosemary took a menacing step in his direction. "Because the drugging part wasn't bad enough."

"You know what?" I stepped out of the way and waved both Griffin and Killian on. "Beat the living shit out of him. If he isn't going to talk or doesn't know anything useful, we might as well at least get even." I prayed that he didn't call my bluff.

"What? No!" Carter lifted a hand in front of his body— like that would save him. "There's no need to beat me up. I didn't mean for any of this to happen."

"How so?" I lifted my chin and stared down my nose at

him. "You stuck me in the neck with a needle and injected something into my bloodstream. That seems pretty purposeful to me."

He took a step toward me. "Dove—"

"Shut up," Griffin bellowed and shoved him in the chest. "Don't even say her name."

"I didn't have a choice." Carter's bottom lip quivered.

Killian shook his head. "You always have a choice. You happened to make the wrong one."

"They have Randall," Carter said. "And they threatened to hurt him if I didn't help them get Dove."

"Randall?" I hadn't heard of anyone by that name.

"His younger brother." Killian sighed, but the tension didn't leave his body. "What do you mean they have him? As in they still do? Why the hell wouldn't you tell me or Billy?"

It took me a second to remember Billy was the pack beta who was stepping into the alpha role while Killian figured things out.

"I was told not to alert anyone—I couldn't risk it. They said that he'd be released once Dove got to wherever the hell they wanted her to go." Carter waved a hand toward me as he continued, "And I'm pretty sure this isn't where they wanted her."

"She got away." Griffin gritted his teeth. "No thanks to you."

"What was I supposed to do?" Carter asked, as his shoulders sagged. "They were going to hurt my brother. Correction... They *are* going to hurt him."

"Why didn't you come to me?" Killian clenched his hands into fists.

"I didn't want to get you tangled up in this." Carter blew out a breath. "I mean, you already lost your entire family. I didn't want to make you choose between Randall and Dove."

"She's my fucking *mate*." Griffin stepped in front of me. "Did you think that we would just be like, 'oh well, it sucks that we lost her?'"

"In my defense, I thought she was still with Killian when I agreed the day before," Carter said, wringing his hands.

"That's a very weak defense." Sierra wrinkled her nose, looking disgusted. "It shouldn't matter whether she's Killian's girlfriend or Griffin's mate."

"It kind of does." Carter ran his fingers through his hair and yanked on the ends. "I knew she wasn't Killian's mate, so he would get over her. When she walked in with Griffin yesterday, it completely threw me, but I was already in too deep. Randall is a good kid. He doesn't deserve to be hurt."

"And she does?" Griffin asked, shoving Carter.

"No, that's not what I meant." Carter plastered himself against the wall. "But he's my *family*."

I understood that all too well. If there had been a way I could've saved my parents or pack, I'd have been tempted to play along, too. Granted, I would've tried to find a way so no one else would've gotten hurt, but Carter clearly didn't have leadership potential. He wasn't an omega, but he definitely wasn't dominant; he did well managing the coffee shop, but his wolf was submissive. "Let's give him the benefit of the doubt." It was hard saying those words, but if I didn't, Griffin wouldn't calm down. "He made the best choice he thought he could under bad circumstances. Whoever we're up against is smart; think about how they managed to take out those four guards that disappeared at the start of the fight two days ago with us none the wiser."

"That doesn't make it okay." Griffin sneered. "He deserves to have his ass beat."

"Maybe, but this gives us a strategic advantage." I had to put on my fighter hat. Making smart choices was the only way we could get a step ahead of the enemy; we were in the dark right now. I faced Killian and Griffin. "Were we able to glean anything from the boat that was left behind?"

"No." Killian sat on the other end of the couch. "There was no registration or anything personal on it."

"That's how the car they used to kidnap me was, too." We'd left the car on the side of the road for someone to find. Hiding it would have raised more questions. "So I'm betting the boat and car were stolen, which strengthens my case for recruiting Carter to help us."

"How can that ding-a-ling help us?" Sierra leaned forward.

"Because they have leverage over him, and he's already proven that he's willing to do whatever it takes to save his brother." I gestured to Killian. "Even going against his alpha and the Shadow City alpha as well."

"In fairness, he doesn't think of me as his alpha." Killian pursed his lips. "I mean, I haven't really been alpha material."

"Well, it's time for that to officially change." If we were going to figure this out, we were all going to have to do things we didn't want to—like me being here, facing the death of my pack—Griffin and Killian were going to have to step up and be the leaders they'd been afraid of being. "We need to pool our resources to have a fighting chance...unless you two want to walk away?" I had to give them an out. This wasn't something they'd ever wanted, and I was asking a lot.

"That question has to be a joke." Griffin's irises darkened. "You're my fated mate. I'm not going anywhere."

"And you're my family now." Killian nodded. "We're all in, and we're going to figure this out together."

"It's about damn time that you two finally step up." Rosemary placed a hand on her hip. "There's been so much turmoil, between your families dying and you two messing around instead of taking charge. You committing to your alpha roles should, at least, cause tensions to die down among the Shadow City representatives."

"You know, sometimes it'd be nice if I could at least wonder what you might be thinking." Griffin scowled at the angel. "But you've never given me the opportunity."

"Sorry if I've ruined your fragile ego several times now." She flipped her hair over her shoulder. "But no one dares to give it to you straight, so I figured I would."

Dear God, I didn't want to listen to their bickering right now. "The point I was trying to get at is they'll wind up calling Carter again to help them out."

"You think so?" Carter cleared his throat and pulled at his collar. "I mean, you're okay with being captured again?"

"No, idiot." Rosemary huffed. "You're not actually going to go through with it."

"But my brother—"

"You're going to tell Killian—using the pack link or whatever—and we'll set it up so we catch whoever is there to collect me, instead of them actually taking me." I had to be careful or he might not be willing to help us. Instead, he could tell whomever it was that we were on to him. "How did they get a hold of you the first time?"

"Some robotic voice called my cell phone." Carter tapped his foot. "Randall must have given them the number. It told me that since you worked at the coffee shop, I got to be the lucky person to help them."

That was what I'd figured. They'd been watching me

and knew that Killian and Griffin wouldn't turn me in; the only other person who had influence over me was my manager. "So, you'll be that lucky person again—which means Carter needs to get back to the coffee shop before they suspect anything." I looked at Rosemary.

"I... I can't risk Randall." Carter slumped over. "If something happens to him—"

I was trying to be nice, but it was time to lay it out for him. "They aren't going to give up your brother willingly. In fact, once you deliver on your end of the bargain, he's as good as dead."

"But they said—"

"They lied," Rosemary interjected. "They've gone out of their way to make sure no one can identify them and that they can't be located. Do you really think they're going to just hand him over if he has any sort of clue who they are? They definitely won't if he's seen some of their faces. The only reason he's still alive is to manipulate you into compliance."

I appreciated that Rosemary had said it instead of me. She had an excellent bad-cop approach, which helped me appeal to Carter's softer side. She and I made a good team. "So, if you help us, we can capture whoever shows up to get me, and we can locate your brother before it's too late."

"Do you believe this?" Carter asked, looking at Killian. "Do you think my brother is at risk?"

"Yes, I do," Killian said curtly. "That's why you should've come to me from the very beginning. Not only would St— Dove be okay, but we could have already gotten Randall back."

I felt bad for Carter. He hadn't known what to do, and he had put so many people at risk. We were all being hard on him, but he needed to learn the lesson.

"Let me be very clear," Griffin said, as he grabbed Carter by the neck. "If you make *any* sort of decision that puts my mate in harm's way again, you will suffer immensely. I don't care what it takes; I'll make sure you go through hell. Do you understand?"

Carter's face turned red, and he nodded his head, as if unable to speak.

"I want to hear you say it." Griffin rasped.

"I..." Carter coughed a few times. "I understand."

Griffin released his hold, and Carter fell back, inhaling sharply.

"Do you mind taking him back?" I asked Rosemary. I didn't want to tell her to do it because that would just irritate her. I needed to be diplomatic in order to keep the angel on our side.

"Yeah, but if he screams the whole way back like he did here, I can't promise I won't drop him." She rubbed her temples. "He gave me a headache."

"Huh." Sierra blew a raspberry. "Can supernaturals get headaches? I never heard someone complain about one."

"This was a first for me." Rosemary reached the door and paused. "So, I'm guessing if we're around someone super annoying, it is possible. Something I wished I hadn't learned firsthand. I might need ear plugs."

Her dramatics were exactly what I needed at the moment. The corner of my mouth tipped upward. "Sorry, I'm fresh out."

"Damn tragedy." She snorted and shook her head.

"Uh...maybe you guys can blindfold me and take me by car." Carter put his hands together like he was in prayer. "Then Rosemary won't have to go through the torture of carrying me."

"You've already been gone too long." They did need to leave, and now. "She'll get you there faster."

"Just come on." Rosemary marched over to him and grabbed him by the ear. "I'll take him back. Call me if you need anything else."

"Ow," Carter whined, as he followed behind Rosemary and out the front door. When it closed, the four of us looked at each other.

"Do you think he'll be able to pull it off?" Sierra tapped a finger against her bottom lip. "I mean, he seems nervous."

"He'll have to if he wants his brother to survive." That was a cold, hard fact—whether we liked it or not.

Killian puffed his cheeks. "He'll be able to pull it off. He loves his family and will do whatever he can to protect his brother. He'd told the pack that Randall had gone on a camping trip, so now it adds up. Randall must be far enough away that we can't use our pack link to connect with him—or he's being drugged. Between that and Carter being willing to face Griffin's and my wrath to do what he thought would save Randall, he'll make it work."

I sure hoped so. "Well, we need to keep digging because, once they call him, we'll have to head back to Shadow Ridge." Luckily, we weren't that far away, but I was afraid to leave before we had searched through everything. There was no telling what we might come back to.

A phone rang from my bedroom. I faced Griffin and said, "You better go answer it."

"It's not mine." He pulled his phone from his pocket.

My stomach dropped. "It's the bear shifter's burner phone." I rushed down the hallway and ran into my room. The phone buzzed on the nightstand and rang for the third time. I snatched it up and pressed the green button.

CHAPTER SEVEN

The line connected, and my stomach dropped. I didn't want to say hello, or they'd know right away something was wrong. They had to already suspect it, or they wouldn't be calling.

Silence filled the line at first, until a deep, menacing voice said, "Samuel, where the fuck are you?"

I'd been afraid the voice would sound familiar, but it didn't. Relief coursed through me that another person I trusted hadn't been working against me. Granted, the two people I trusted most were here with me.

"Samuel?" the man said in a lower tone.

Griffin, Killian, and Sierra entered the room, and we all looked at each other, at a loss as to how to proceed.

What's the plan? Griffin asked as he glared at the phone.

"Who's there?" the man demanded. "I take it the silver wolf is listening."

Sierra's head snapped in my direction, and her mouth dropped open.

Well, there went keeping Sierra in the dark. I only

hoped Killian's judgment was sound with this one...because it hadn't been with Carter.

"For some supposed 'fierce warrior,' you're sure scared to talk to me." The guy chuckled, clearly trying to get a rise out of me.

He already assumes I'm here, so I might as well speak. Maybe I could wrangle some sort of information from him. "I'm not scared, just trying to decide if you're actually worth the effort."

"Ah, I heard that you had a smart mouth." He *tsked.* "Very unbecoming of a lady."

I let disdain drip from each word. "I'm sure I'll lose sleep tonight over disappointing you."

"See, that's what's wrong with having a female who thinks she's destined to be alpha. You don't respect the natural balance of the hierarchy."

No. He *didn't* just go there. "You mean I should be willing to submit to any male wolf?"

"Exactly." He scoffed. "This whole women's rights movement doesn't work, especially in the supernatural world."

This guy was a dick and the exact reason Dad had been so hard on me growing up. Assholes like him had to be put in their place, and I couldn't wait to be the one to teach him that lesson. "Yet, you're the one hiring people to come after me while you stay behind, all safe and snug in your secret hideout."

"There are reasons for that," he growled. "And none of them have to do with me actually being worried that you could best me. There's a lot at stake here, more than you even know."

"All I'm hearing is that you all are too scared to let your identities be known." This situation had been one hot mess after another—along with many different races getting involved—which made it even more complicated.

Maybe you shouldn't goad him? Griffin frowned, as concern flowed from him through our mate bond.

He wanted to protect me, but this person wasn't going to stop. Whether I spoke to him or not, whoever was behind this would continue to come for me. They had this grand plan that centered around me; they wanted to control the silver wolf population. We had to figure out the end game— if we could do that, it should help us determine who might be pulling the strings. *If I anger him enough, he might reveal something, or react without thinking. It's the best strategy we have right now.*

"We aren't scared, and our identities will come out sooner rather than later." The guy sounded amused, not angry. "I applaud your efforts to rile me up. However, you have no clue what you're up against. If you're free, that means Samuel failed, which is unacceptable. Death is a blessing compared to the punishment he would have received for coming back empty-handed."

The reference to Samuel killing himself was clear. This guy was feeling me out—trying to determine if the bear shifter had given up anything. I wouldn't let him know that the bear shifter wasn't alive any longer.

"Noted." I inhaled sharply. "I'll relay the message to Samuel for you."

"Oh, is he near?" His tone took on an edge. "I'd love to hear his voice to confirm he's still alive."

"Why would I do you any favors?" He was calling my bluff. We were in a game of chess where we were trying to outsmart one another.

"Because I don't believe you have him." The guy chuckled. "He's too smart to do something that would negatively impact his family. Well, this conversation has been fun, but I've got other pressing things to attend to. I'll talk to you soon."

Now the bear being desperate enough to kill himself made sense. He'd been protecting his family, just as Carter was trying to protect his brother. Whoever we were up against was heartless and cruel. They didn't mind taking whoever they needed to in order to get their pawns to comply. Though, I imagined the bear shifter's family *wasn't* safe. We needed to locate these assholes so we could free everyone they'd taken prisoner.

Before my finger hit the red hang-up button, the guy spoke again, "Oh, and Sterlyn."

The fact that he dropped my name made me uneasy. He was about to say something that would trip me up. My gut screamed a warning, but there wasn't a damn thing I could do. "Yeah?"

"Tell the Shadow City alpha and the Shadow Ridge alpha that I said hi." He ended the call; the silence was harsh—a screaming in my ear.

He wanted the shock value, and he'd gotten it.

"There were so many things wrong with that conversation." Sierra walked past me and paced in front of my bed. "No one thought it might be a good idea to tell me that Sterlyn is a fucking silver wolf?"

"No one was supposed to find out. Only Atticus was supposed to know we still existed." I had no idea how this group had found out about us, but being slaughtered and attacked reaffirmed that our ancestors were right to have hidden us. We'd wanted no part of the corruption that had taken over the supernatural world. We'd kept to ourselves and stayed peaceful so that others wouldn't try to use us as pawns.

Guess that hadn't worked out so well.

"Everyone thought the silver wolf was a myth." Sierra shook her head. "You're one of the strongest supernatural beings there are, which is why these people want to capture you. But why did they kill off the entire pack? You'd think they would want to control all the silver wolves."

There was no use keeping things hidden from her at this point. She knew my secret, so I might as well fill in the gaps —especially since she was in harm's way now. "Because we could kill them if we decided to fight, and my father would refuse to work with them."

"Then why not kill you, too?" She waved her hands like she had a sword. "It doesn't make sense."

"They plan to use me as a breeder." A shiver ran down my spine as Sierra gasped. "And break me so I'll submit to whoever is in charge."

"Which is never going to happen." Griffin pulled me against his chest and wrapped his arms around me.

"He purposely dropped that he knew Griffin and I were with you." Killian cracked his knuckles as he nibbled on his bottom lip. "Which means someone must have realized we found you."

I hadn't considered that. The thought sat like a hard lump in my stomach. "You're right. We probably need to get back to Shadow Ridge soon since they could see if we were hiding here." But there were still some spots unturned in my dad's office. "Let's finish searching the house. Maybe Killian and Sierra could keep an eye out to make sure no one comes through before we're ready to go."

"Yeah, we should probably get out there now, after that call." Killian stepped into the hallway and looked at Sierra. "Let's warm up the leftover pizza and load Sterlyn's things into the vehicles. That way, if someone comes, we can leave."

"Let me pack some stuff." There was no reason to leave here without my clothes and personal items. It would save me a ton of money.

"Sounds like a plan," Sierra said, as she followed Killian down the hallway.

Sighing, I grabbed two duffel bags from under my bed and began filling them with all of the essential things I needed.

"DID YOU FIND ANYTHING?" Griffin asked, as he slammed the drawer to the last cabinet he'd searched through in my dad's office.

"No." I'd dug through the entire desk multiple times, hoping to find *something* that could hint to who could be behind the attacks, but nothing looked even a little bit promising. Most of it was bills and a few piddly things that had to do with the land surrounding us. As I'd guessed, the town's land had been passed down over generations, and he had several offers from people wanting to purchase it from us.

"That's so strange." Griffin glanced around the walls. "Dad's office was like this too. He handled a lot of political stuff, but when Mom and I looked through his files, it was like he hadn't kept any paperwork on the packs and Shadow City."

"Well, he knew where we were located. The knowledge had to pass down somehow." My gut said there had to be something that had gone unfound or was missing. Dad was paranoid—always thinking about ways to hide things in case something happened—and we were found; that told me that he had information secretly hidden somewhere. We had lived here for centuries—something of importance *had* to have been kept here, somewhere.

"At the time I didn't know that...but yeah, exactly." Griffin stood behind me and rubbed my shoulders. "You're tense."

"Being drugged and kidnapped after losing your entire pack will do that to you," I bit out, and immediately regretted being a bitch to him. None of this was his fault, but my nerves were frayed. "I'm sorry. I have no right to talk to you that way." I was also on edge from expecting Killian to call at any moment telling us to move, but luckily, he hadn't. We had at least a little more time to look—I just didn't know where else to search.

"Hey, it's okay." He kissed my forehead as his fingers dug deeper, working out the knots.

The pressure both hurt and felt amazing, relaxing me enough to clear my mind. "Maybe we're thinking about this all wrong." If I knew Dad like I thought I did, he wouldn't leave information where someone could easily find it. He'd leave enough—like the land offers—to make people think that was all there was.

Like I almost had.

Griffin's hands stilled. "He'd have a hidden compartment or location."

"Exactly." But where the hell would that be? I looked around the room for something that seemed a little out of place.

Nothing stood out.

"Maybe it's not in this room." Griffin dropped his hands. "This would be kind of a dead giveaway location-wise, right?"

"I bet it'd be in their bedroom." I had avoided going into their room so far, but fate kept nudging me that way. She must have a sick sense of humor.

"Do you want me to look?" Griffin squeezed my arm. "You don't have to go in there if you don't want to."

The fact that I would love to take him up on the offer proved that this was something I had to do. "Yeah, but I'm going with you." I wouldn't have been strong enough to do it on my own.

"Are you sure?" Griffin tucked a stray piece of my hair behind my ear. "I don't mind looking alone if you aren't ready."

"I can't keep letting their deaths impact me this much." I would never get over losing them, but I had to face reality. "Otherwise, these guys will continue to have leverage over me, and that's not acceptable."

"You're stronger than anyone I've ever known," he whispered, placing a hand on my cheek. "You make me want to be a better man."

I couldn't keep the giggle from bubbling out. "Really? You're going that cheesy?"

"Any other girl would've loved to hear words like that from me." He lifted his chin, pretending to be upset. "But not you. You always make me work for it, even when I mean what I say."

"No, that's sweet." Even though he was trying to keep our conversation lighthearted, I could feel a little bit of hurt wafting through our bond. "I'm sorry. I just never thought I'd hear you say something like that, especially since the first time you spoke to me, you informed me you only liked your cream in one place."

He grimaced and closed his eyes. "Please don't remind me of that. That was definitely not my finest moment."

"No, it definitely was not." I pecked him on the lips and smiled. "And yet, here we are."

"I wouldn't trade it for anything," he said, as he winked and took my hand. "Come on, let's go see if we can find anything."

The moment of lightheartedness vanished, and I followed his lead. We did need to finish our search.

I headed to the very last doorway in the hall. My hands grew sweaty as I reached for the doorknob. I wasn't ready for this—I never would be. I was going to have to push through.

Trying not to overthink it, I opened the door. My parents' bed was made, the navy-blue comforter, wrinkle-free, contrasted with the white bed frame. The sky-blue walls made the room feel too bright for the staggering hole they'd left behind. My heart fractured further, feeling the pain of their loss even more in the moment.

"Any idea where they would hide something?" Griffin entered the room, running his hand along the wall.

"No." But at least there weren't any cabinets or desks to go through.

I scanned the room, trying to think like my dad. He was always so straightforward and said what he meant.

Griffin walked around the room, stepping purposefully on various parts of the floor. He listened to the noises the floorboards made, trying to find a spot that sounded more hollow. He bent over and knocked on a low portion of the wall. His gray boxers peeked out from his jeans.

Some of Dad's words of wisdom played inside my brain. He'd always told me that people's underwear drawers held the best secrets; that they could tell you more about a person than anything else. I'd always thought the comment was odd and would roll my eyes, exclaiming he was weird.

Wait.

What if that had been a clue? I might be losing my mind, but...at this point, what did we have to lose?

I rushed to his chest of drawers. The underwear drawer was at the very bottom. I pulled it open, then moved his boxers out of the way.

Gross. I tried not to think about touching my father's underwear as the bottom of the drawer came into view. I inhaled sharply as the outline of a hidden compartment became visible. Had I not been looking for it, I would've missed it. With a shaky hand, I dug my fingernails into one side and lifted.

I couldn't believe my eyes. Documents and a photo album sat inside.

Griffin's phone rang, startling me back to the present.

"It's Killian," he rasped as he answered the phone. "Hello?"

"There are cars heading this way," Killian yelled.

CHAPTER EIGHT

Dammit. They'd figured out that we were here—but how? My first thought was Carter, but it didn't feel right. He'd seemed genuinely sorry for betraying me, but maybe that was remorse for being caught instead of for helping me get kidnapped.

I could stew on the how later. The looming threat was all that mattered right now. We had to get out of here without any more deaths, and before the enemy trapped us.

"How many vehicles are there?" Griffin asked as he stepped over next to me.

"Four huge SUVs. You two need to get out and into your car, now—they'll be here in minutes. We're heading your way."

Of course, they were. At least I'd found Dad's stash, even though it would've been nice to figure out the riddle earlier; we could've bypassed this encounter. Thankfully, we weren't leaving empty-handed. "I think I've found what we were looking for." It'd be nice to confirm it by looking through the stuff, but we didn't have time. I had to trust my instinct. Dad wouldn't have hidden something if he didn't think it was valuable.

"Why am I not surprised?" Griffin kissed my cheek, as he glanced around the room. "You're kind of amazing. Let's find something to put it in."

"Let's not go overboard with the compliments." I was definitely not amazing—if I were, we wouldn't be in our current situation. I stood and picked up the drawer. "And we don't have time to pack it. We're taking it as is." I rushed out the door and headed down the hallway. Thankfully, the vehicles were already loaded, so we just needed to get in and go.

Griffin followed me, and I heard the jangle of the keys as he pulled them from his pocket.

As I entered the living room, the front door opened, and Killian's strained face appeared. He glanced at the drawer and then at Griffin and me. "Come on. They're pulling into the neighborhood now."

"Do we know how many there are?" I jogged past him and stepped outside.

I glanced at his truck, finding Sierra in the driver's seat. Her hands clutched the wheel, and her chest heaved with each breath. She looked petrified, and I kind of hated that Killian had included her in our mess.

They'd lump her in with me now, which meant there was no telling what the enemy would do to her family. It was clear that they weren't above hurting or abusing inno-cent people to get what they wanted.

Enough people had been hurt or threatened because of me, and I hated to add another person to the ever-growing list.

"I have no clue," Killian answered as Griffin ran outside.

Griffin pressed the unlock button on his key fob and the

car doors clicked. I rushed to open the passenger door and set the drawer on the floorboard. Fortunately, the vehicles hadn't turned down the dead-end road yet and hadn't seen that we'd carried something out, and they probably wouldn't be looking for anything in the car.

"Let's go," Griffin commanded as he hurried to the driver's side door and opened it. He leaned over the seat like he was searching for something.

The sounds of engines rumbled, and the vehicles took the turn and rushed toward us. One of the windows rolled down, and the barrel of a gun poked out, aiming in our direction.

Shit. We would be huge targets in the vehicles.

"We need to go into the woods." Everything inside me screamed to get into the car and go, but the protector side knew it was a horrible idea. If we tried, they would blow out our tires, and then we'd be even more at their mercy. I couldn't let panic take over. "Otherwise, we're sitting ducks. The trees will offer some protection."

As if reinforcing my words, the gun fired, and a bullet hit the back tire of Killian's truck. Air poured out as the vehicle drooped.

"Dammit." Killian opened the passenger door and yelled, "Sierra, crawl over here and get out *now.*"

Don't press the lock button on the fob, or they'll wonder why we cared enough to lock the vehicle. I pressed the lock button on the inside of the door panel so the horn wouldn't beep, and then slammed it shut.

Griffin shut the driver's door and ran toward me. He took my hand and tugged me toward the trees. "We've got to move."

The tires squealed as the vehicles came to a harsh stop.

We were about to run out of time. Killian and Sierra ran past the Navigator, and Griffin and I ran hard behind them.

A few shots were fired and hit the ground beside us, breaking up dirt.

We ran at an angle, using our cars for coverage. Car doors opened as the enemies climbed out in hot pursuit.

At least I was on land that I knew all too well. Worst case—if we had to—we could run all the way back to Shadow Ridge, but that would be hard with the four of us. When I had been alone, they'd almost caught me. With four of us, it would be a miracle if we all got away.

A loud *caw* sounded overhead, and I looked into the sky to find a black crow hovering there. It paused directly over me, flapping like it was taunting me. It held a branch in its talons and dropped it, making a faint *crack*. The crow cawed again, mocking me.

Dammit, we hadn't been alone when we'd arrived here, after all. That branch I'd heard must have been the crow. I'd been so focused on a threat at ground level that I hadn't thought about looking in the damn trees. I should've known better, but the emotional strain of being here had gotten the better of me—that was why I hadn't sensed anything out of the ordinary. The bird had been God knew how high in the sky, so I couldn't smell it.

At least that told me that whoever it was didn't live close by. Granted, they'd have to take time to group and get here, but if they lived in a city close by, they would've gotten here during the night.

Killing that dumbass bird jumped even higher on my priority list. He had flown under the radar way too many times, but I wouldn't make that mistake again. At least, Carter hadn't betrayed us again. That was the silver lining, if there was one.

"We all need to split up," one of the enemies commanded. "Remember, do not kill the girl, but stop her by any means necessary."

So in other words, shoot, but not to kill.

"What about the other three?" another man asked, bullets jangling as he loaded his gun.

"They don't matter," the first man responded. "Our mission is to get the girl."

Follow me. At some point, we would need to split up—but right now, I needed to get us far enough away that we all could talk. The first priority was getting past the crow.

I took off running deeper into the woods. A small cave sat about four hundred yards away that we should be able to use for shelter for at least a little while.

The three of them ran after me. I zigzagged, hoping to confuse the crow. Its wings flapped overhead, confirming what I already knew...it was tracking us to alert the idiots.

We were going to have to split up. We couldn't shake the crow.

Coming to a stop, I faced the other three and spoke quietly. We'd gained enough distance from our pursuers that if we talked softly enough, they wouldn't be able to hear. "We need to split up. That damn crow is following us. I'd hoped to hide out in a nearby cave for a little while until their group split up to look for us, but that won't work."

"So, what do we do?" Sierra asked with trepidation.

I took a deep breath so I wouldn't snap at her. It was clear that the only one besides myself with any sort of training was Killian. But Sierra was here, trying to help, and I had to remember that. She was definitely proving her loyalty. "First off, what weapons do we have?" I bent and pulled my knife from my ankle sheath.

"Even though I didn't want to, I did bring something

when you went missing." Killian lifted his shirt, revealing a gun.

If I wasn't mated to Griffin and didn't consider Killian a brother, I would've kissed him right then. I'd expected to be the only one with a weapon. "Anyone else?"

"Believe it or not, me too." Griffin pulled out a gun from his waistband. "I'm learning that, when it comes to you, we all need to be prepared."

"What?" I couldn't believe my eyes. "How the hell did I not know you had that on you?" We'd had sex the night before, and he hadn't had it then. It was like it appeared out of thin air.

"It was in the Navigator," he said with pride. "That's why I opened the door in the first place."

We actually had a better chance with two guns. The men tracking us wouldn't expect that, based on the last several fights they'd had with us. We'd never had guns in the pack before; only the handful of our guards that they'd taken out had carried them.

"Do you know how to shoot?" I didn't mean to come off condescending. Griffin was a strong wolf and a good fighter in animal form...the problem was when he was in human form. He didn't have strong skills then—although, that one punch he'd given Carter had shown good form.

"Yes...believe it or not, I do." Griffin sighed. "I didn't grow up training for battle, only politics, but the Shadow City leaders are all about target practice for leisure."

I'd take any wins we could get. "Okay, then let's split into two groups." I'd initially thought we'd all four separate, but that would be too risky—especially with Sierra weaponless. Killian was a trained fighter, so it made sense for her to go with him. "Griffin and I will stay together. You two head off that way." I pointed in the direction we'd been heading. "If you stay straight, it'll take you to a cave that you can use for cover. If you go to the side where the opening backs up to a wall, there's a section that's covered all around except for in front of you. You can use it to keep these guys at bay."

"What about you two?" Killian frowned. "We could all go there together."

"The cave isn't large enough for all four of us." We didn't have time to debate everything. "And if they stay grouped together, they can strategize more. If they split up, they can't make as much of a coordinated effort. You've gotta assume they have tranquilizer guns and can mind link. We can't."

"She knows the area and is a fucking silver wolf. She was born for this kind of thing." Sierra took a step in the direction I'd indicated. "And the longer we stay here, the faster they'll find us."

"Fine, but text us if you get in trouble." Killian hugged me tightly. "And please don't get captured." His body was rigid with tension and concern.

"Same to you two." I returned the embrace.

The sound of footsteps broke the moment. The enemy was coming, and faster than I'd given them credit for. Not willing to speak again, I gestured toward the cave.

Killian nodded and patted Griffin on the back before taking off. He and Sierra kept in step with each other as they ran in the direction I'd told them to.

Any ideas for us? Griffin held the gun at his side with his finger on the trigger.

I moved southward, away from Killian and Sierra, making sure our enemies would hear us and split. Even though I was their end goal, they'd have to keep an eye on the other two. No fighter would ignore two people who could be threats. *Unfortunately, there isn't a spot like that for us. We're going to have to run so they'll at least split up, and then fight.*

As if they'd figured out our plan, their footsteps paused, and the leader spoke quietly, "They split up. It's clear the silver wolf went that way, so let's separate. This half goes with me, and the rest of you follow Bo's lead."

They were speaking out loud, which made me think that maybe they weren't pack, either. At least this put us on more equal grounds.

"Got it," a guy responded, and half the group moved in the opposite direction from us.

"From here on out, we don't talk," the leader commanded. "We need to be as quiet as possible to try to surprise them." The group took off again, but they were noisier, probably because they didn't know the terrain. Luckily, they wouldn't get the drop on us.

Is there a way we can round them up or lock them in somewhere? Griffin kept pace with me.

I wished there was somewhere like that, but it was going to be hand-to-hand combat. *We can get to the river so no one can sneak up behind us. I could maybe shift and have them focus on me so you can pick them off one at a time.*

In other words, use you as bait? Griffin's anger was palpable through the bond. *Hell, no. Unacceptable. Absolutely not.*

The problem was this wasn't up for debate. *They're gunning for me...the rest of you are collateral damage. We have to think strategically. If we dangle me in front of them, they'll be more focused on capturing me than hurting you. It's our best chance of making it out with minimal injuries.*

Griffin growled. *It sounds like you've already made up your mind.*

Having him upset with me didn't sit well. This was our

first disagreement, but I knew using me as bait was our best and safest strategy. I owed it to all of us to take the least risky approach. *If things get too dicey, I promise to shift back to human and fight alongside you.*

The suggestion seemed to appease the beast, and his anger receded. *Okay. I'm not thrilled with this suggestion, but I trust you. If you think this is best, I'll go along with it. Just...please don't make me regret it.*

My heart warmed. *Thank you. I'm going to shift now, but take my knife so I don't lose it.*

I handed him the knife and sheath, and he put it in his pocket.

The sound of our pursuers' feet hadn't gotten any closer —probably because they were moving slower, making sure they kept on our trail. They hadn't caught wind of us yet, which was miraculous.

Not bothering to strip, I called my wolf forward. She obliged willingly, sensing the trouble we were in.

My bones cracked as I shifted from human to wolf, and my skin tingled as fur sprouted all over my body. My clothes ripped away, and soon I stood on four legs.

A loud *caw* grated on my nerves, followed by the flapping of wings.

I lifted my head to see the crow flying over us, making enough racket that the enemy wolves would be able to find us. He hadn't made that move until I shifted, which meant he knew I was up to something.

I'd hoped to be closer to the water before they picked up our trail. *I can't wait to kill that bird. Maybe you can shoot it.*

It would be my pleasure. Griffin kept pace beside me.

If we ever got some downtime and I could work with Griffin, he would be an excellent fighter in both wolf and human form. Maybe when we got out of this horrible situation, I'd demand we take time for him to train. It'd be good for both of us—it would help me maintain my skills, and he would learn some important moves that would help in situations like this one.

The enemy heard us and moved faster, as if not worried about sneaking up on us anymore.

We weren't going to make it to the water, but we at least knew no one was circling around us. I stopped running and turned in the direction they would appear.

It was time to fight, and I prayed that Griffin was a good shot.

CHAPTER NINE

T he enemy was close enough that I could hear each intake of breath. Being in wolf form amplified my senses, and I could make out ten distinct gaits that raced toward us.

Killian was right about the numbers. I was mildly impressed that he'd read the situation so accurately—I wouldn't have been correct if someone had asked me to predict how many people would come after us. *Ten are approaching us. With the way they're shuffling, there are two in front, so we'll need to take them out fast. If we do, it should make the others hesitate.*

Okay. Griffin aimed his gun in the direction they would appear. *I've got this,* he reassured me...and himself.

My confidence in his ability faltered, but I held my doubt close, not wanting him to feel it through our bond. If he had to talk himself up, that meant either he wasn't sure he could pull the trigger, or he was that inexperienced. Either way, doubt was dangerous in war, and whether we liked it or not, these battles were leading up to just that.

I threw my head back and howled. The enemy felt invigorated and in control; they knew their numbers and weapons exceeded ours. We had to hit fast and hard to show them that we weren't afraid at all.

As expected, their pace slowed. They hadn't expected me to alert them to where we were, and I'd thrown them off.

Good, my plan was already working.

"At least one of them has shifted," one of the men whispered, but he might as well have spoken in his normal voice. "Do you think it's her?" His voice raised in trepidation.

"Shhh," the leader hissed and slowed down.

One of the enemies was scared enough to speak out loud, confirming they weren't part of the same pack, which would make the situation even more problematic long-term —but in our current circumstances, it would help.

If multiple packs were working together, they'd have more resources at their disposal. That thought made my stomach sour. At some point, we had to get on even ground with them. They knew a whole hell of a lot about me, but I knew very little about them. If we wanted a chance at succeeding, we needed to figure all this out...and fast.

The crow flew several feet above my head, making a ton of noise. He was giving away my exact location. That bird was the gift that kept on giving. I couldn't wait to return the favor. I still relished the idea of plucking out each feather, one by one. After all of the pain and suffering he'd put us through, that kind of torture seemed fitting.

The footsteps sped up now that they had a little bit going in their favor again.

That damn bird has got to go, Griffin rasped.

A loud gunshot rang out, and the crow screeched before dropping. His dead body fell right in front of my face, landing mere inches from my body.

Holy shit. Griffin had shot the bastard...and he'd hit him on the first try. He was a good shot, after all.

Comforted that we might have a chance, I focused on the trees the enemies would soon be crashing through. I was a little disappointed that I hadn't been the one to kill the crow, but at least he was dead. That definitely leveled the playing field.

The enemy was upon us, and the first one stepped through the trees. I growled, bringing his attention to me and not Griffin. The fur at my ruff stood up as I let every bit of my anger shine through.

He swung the gun at me, aiming for my shoulder, but Griffin shot immediately—the bullet hitting between the man's eyes. He fell hard with a resounding thud.

"What the—" someone gasped from behind the tree.

"Don't just stand there," another one said, *"move."*

Chaos descended among them, and two men charged into the area.

Knowing they would be looking for the gun, I lunged toward them, forcing them to pay attention to me. One guy tripped over the man who was already dead, as the second guy swung his gun toward me and pulled the trigger.

Move right! Griffin yelled, and I listened, jumping to the side.

The bullet missed me by inches, and Griffin fired two shots, one after another, each hitting its mark. Both were kill-shots in the same place as the first. Griffin had taken out three men.

"What do we do?" one guy blubbered.

"Attack, dumbass," the leader barked. "Now!"

Get behind a tree and use it as coverage, because they're going to try to take you out now. I needed to know he was protected. I pivoted in his direction as Griffin raced behind the largest nearby tree. Most of his body was covered—the only part visible, his hand holding the gun.

Three more enemies stumbled toward us, and, as I'd suspected, neither glanced my way. That worked, too, because I could get closer and take a few out. If we injured them to the point of not fighting, we could get the hell out of here.

I wished there was a way to handle this without killing, but if Griffin didn't shoot to kill, we'd be overrun in seconds. My dad always told me that the fact that we didn't relish killing made the silver wolves different...and after going through all I had, I agreed. I couldn't kill that bear shifter when he was lying on the ground all vulnerable; I couldn't kill maliciously like that. Granted, he still wound up dead, but that was a whole different scenario.

The taller of the three had his gun aimed at Griffin the quickest, which meant he was the one I needed to take out. He fired a shot at my mate before Griffin could respond.

Are you okay? I asked, as I lunged at the guy's gun hand. The other four men were already moving in this direction, probably realizing that coming one by one was allowing us to pick them off more easily.

Griffin fired as he responded. *Yes, thank God you told me to get behind the tree.*

The taller guy looked at me right as my teeth sank into his wrist. His eyes widened as he yanked his arm back, but it was too late; he released his hold on the gun, and it fell. His other hand came around and punched my face, causing my jaw to slacken enough for him to pull his wrist out.

I snarled as his blood dripped down my chin. My jaw throbbed, but with my shifter healing, I'd be better within minutes. All I needed to do was weaken as many of them as I could so Griffin could take them out.

Arms wrapped my neck with the butt of a gun digging into my throat as another enemy attacked me. He tightened his arms, trying to cut off my oxygen. I grew dizzy, and if I didn't get out of his hold soon, I'd faint.

Extending the claws on my hind legs, I kicked the asshole in the stomach, digging the nails in as deep as I could get them to go.

He grunted in pain and released his hold. I slashed his skin as I stood back on four legs, and the guy tripped over a tree root and fell. With shaky arms, he raised his gun, and my instincts took over. I bit into his neck, ripping it out.

His body convulsed before going limp.

My heart hurt, but I didn't allow myself to whimper or show any regret. The others would attempt to use my sympathetic side to their advantage, and they didn't need more leverage.

Gunshots fired as our last four enemies joined the fight. I scanned the area to find one left from the last batch locked on Griffin. There was a total of five who were still standing, and they were coordinating their attack.

Instead of attacking just one, I needed to cause pandemonium and swipe at everyone. That way, all of them would have to keep an eye on me.

Unsure what I was going to do, I tried not to overthink it. I charged at each man, running into them before moving on to the next. I kicked my legs and bucked my body, imitating a bull.

All of my years of training had officially been flushed down the toilet.

Griffin continued to fire as I distracted as many of them as I could.

"What the hell is she doing?" the leader grumbled as I

kicked a leg higher and hit his face. My claws slashed his cheek, and blood welled up.

"You stupid bitch," he spat and swung the butt of his gun toward my head.

Nope...I already got nailed there once, and it still hurt. I wouldn't allow myself to be injured a second time. I threw my body into his, which made the gun miss my head— barely—but his forearm hit me instead. It hurt, but not nearly as bad as if it had been metal.

Lowering my head even more, I bulldozed the leader into one of the tree trunks.

Duck, Griffin commanded.

Obeying, I dropped and looked upward as his gun fired. A bullet buzzed over my head and into the leader's heart. He jerked as his eyes widened. He glanced at his chest and then focused on me. He lifted his gun, ready to shoot me— but then his head bobbled to the side, and he slumped against the tree.

I spun around to find my next target and realized that there was only one remaining. The guy must have noticed the same thing because he turned and ran back in the direction they'd come from.

No, we couldn't let him get away—we might get some answers out of him. I chased after him, and he glanced over his shoulder at me. Seeing that I was catching up, his face hardened in determination. He reached for his belt buckle, and I knew exactly what he was going to do.

The same thing that damn bear shifter did. He even kept it in the same place.

I pushed my legs harder, urging myself to get to him before he took the damn pill. Once he got it in his mouth, there was no taking it back.

He spun around and fired. The bullet lodged in my shoulder. My leg crumpled underneath me, and I skidded into the ground.

I howled and linked with Griffin, *He's about to kill himself.*

What? Griffin sounded surprised. *I'm hurrying.*

But he wouldn't get there in time.

I forced myself to stand, my leg throbbing with sharp, excruciating pain. But I somehow managed to hobble toward him.

"I'm so sorry, but I had no choice." The enemy put the pill in his mouth and a tear dripped down his face. "You have no clue who you're up against."

Ugh. I wanted to ask questions, but I was in animal form and couldn't communicate with him. He seemed like a decent guy who'd been put in an impossible situation. I was beginning to see a common theme.

His body shook as the drug worked into his system. There was no saving him now.

My eyes burned, and my throat constricted with frustration and anger at whoever had created this mess. All of these people we'd killed might not have been here truly willingly, but at the end of the day, their goal was still the same.

Capture me.

Kill the others.

They'd forced us to do whatever was necessary to survive. Letting these men capture me would only make whoever the enemy was stronger and would cause even more unrest and hate to spread throughout our world.

Griffin raced toward me and stopped short when he saw the blood dripping from my shoulder. *I felt you were in pain. What happened?* He dropped to his knees and examined my wound. *Did you get shot?*

Yes, but I'll be fine. It was superficial, but I needed the bullet removed. *Do you have a way to get the bullet out? It's not deep.*

No. His jaw twitched. *I've got nothing but keys and a gun.*

You have my knife. I nodded to his pocket. *Use it and get it out before I heal. It'll hurt worse if we do it later, and if I shift to human with the bullet still inside, it could make my injury worse. I need to shift back to human form now that we have their guns so we can help Killian and Sierra.*

Fine. He placed his gun beside him and pulled out my knife. He inhaled sharply and cracked his neck.

If I wasn't in so much pain, I'd have laughed. He looked as if he was preparing for battle.

He held the knife right at the edge of the entry wound, and I forced myself to look at the fallen man, who had died while we were preoccupied. Bubbles poured out of his mouth and down his face.

On the count of—

Just do it. I didn't want to know when. Anticipation was not my friend right now.

Griffin stuck the knife in, and pain coursed throughout my shoulder. I'd thought getting shot wouldn't hurt much, but I'd been so damn wrong. A whimper escaped me, and I was at the pain's mercy.

The edges of my vision grew dark as Griffin dug around for the bullet.

Maybe I should pull out, he said as he paused.

We've already gotten this far. I took deep breaths, trying to prevent myself from passing out, and attempting to keep nausea at bay. If I got sick, I wouldn't be able to help Killian and Sierra.

Griffin continued his efforts, and his guilt and concern flowed into me, making my already raw emotions even more frayed.

I feel it, he said excitedly. *I've got it.*

Then get it out. I groaned.

He angled the blade—cutting the wound larger—but within seconds, the bullet fell out, and the knife finally exited my body.

I sagged with relief. Even though the pain was still excruciating, it didn't come close to how it'd felt with the knife inside me. *Thank you.*

Let's make a pact that this is the last time you get shot. Griffin rolled the bloody bullet between his fingers while his other hand ran through my fur, making my skin buzz from our connection.

It'd be nice to sit here and enjoy the peace and quiet, but we needed to find Killian and Sierra. We hadn't heard anything from them.

Can you take the guy's shirt off him? I asked. I had ripped my clothes, not considering that we'd have access to extra guns, and I'd need to be able to use one. *I want to shift back so we can grab some of their guns to go help Killian and Sierra...and I'd rather not be completely naked.*

Griffin growled, *Hell no. You're wearing mine.* He pulled his hunter-green shirt from his body as I shifted back into my human form. His abs contracted, making my body warm at a very inappropriate time. I looked away, needing to keep my head on straight and not drool.

When I was on two legs, he helped me put on the shirt without using my injured arm too much. The garment was huge on me, and the hem hit around my knees, much like a dress.

Being shorter came in handy, at least for the moment.

When I felt comfortable, I bent down to pick up the dead man's gun. "Now let's go help our friends."

CHAPTER TEN

I hated the way the gun fit into my hand. Weapons like these went against my animal instincts because they were the opposite of natural. They tore down communities and more, but they were highly effective in battle.

That reason alone was why Dad had trained us with firearms. He had emphasized that learning to fight with them was just as essential as learning to fight without them. He was right...but I hated the fact that we might have to use them again if we were all going to come out of this alive.

I preferred a bow and arrow, but there weren't any on hand, and they were bulkier to carry.

We needed to get to Killian and Sierra, but grabbing a few more guns might be worth taking a few extra minutes. Even though my shoulder throbbed, I pushed through the pain. *Let's go grab another gun each.*

Not waiting for him to respond, I turned and ran back toward the others we'd killed. Griffin ran close behind me, his anxiety flowing through our bond. He probably never expected to go through something like this, and here I'd waltzed into his world, turning his entire life upside down. I couldn't help but think that maybe he would've been better off if we hadn't met. He'd almost died once and was already in another battle—not even three days later. If we hadn't stumbled upon each other, he would probably be sitting at Dick's bar with Killian and Luna, drinking a beer.

Despite the thought being hypothetical, flames of jealousy flickered through me. I hated that Luna had gotten her claws into Griffin for so long. We hadn't seen her since the night she'd shown up drunk at his house, but she had clearly intended to hurt, if not kill me. Had I not caused her to fall into Killian's pool, there was no telling how that confrontation would've ended. Granted, she'd almost drowned because I hadn't realized she was that far gone until it was too late. Killian had jumped in and saved her.

I ran through the last section of trees. Looking at the bodies littered across the ground made my heart hurt, and somehow looked even more gruesome than I remembered. So many of these deaths could've been prevented.

Squatting next to the closest two bodies, I pried the guns from their cool hands—I could already detect the faint smell of decay. Holding my breath, I turned and handed another gun to Griffin while keeping two for myself.

Griffin's fingers brushed my bullet wound.

Blood had soaked through the green shirt in that spot, and there was still an ache, but it was dulling. Silver wolves healed faster than any other shifter, and even faster than vampires when they drank blood. With a wound this deep and irritated, it'd probably take a day or two for it to be completely healed, but I should be able to move without wincing by tonight.

Maybe you should rest. Griffin's eyes deepened to a

brown. *You can head back to the Navigator while I get them out.*

No way in hell would I let that happen. They were still grossly outnumbered, and even though Griffin was an amazing shot, I couldn't, in good conscience, run to safety while the three of them were in danger. *I'm fine. I promise.* I kissed him, taking an extra moment to reassure him. He had been almost panicked with worry ever since I got shot. *It's already not hurting as bad.* I slowly peeled the shirt away from the wound. *See, the bleeding has already slowed.*

In other words, you're refusing to stay behind. Griffin huffed as he caressed my face. *Fine, but if it starts hurting worse or bleeding again, promise me you'll let me take the lead.*

Promise. I couldn't deny him that, as long as I was there with him.

The air remained sulfur-free, which caused him to relax marginally.

Now, let's go. I was chomping to get away from all the dead people, as well as check on Killian and Sierra. If I wasn't worried about their cell phone distracting them or giving away their location, I'd have been texting them now. But we had to go in blind.

We sprinted through the woods in the direction of the cave.

The sound of shots firing echoed all around. I hadn't even noticed that it had been quiet until then. Maybe they weren't in over their heads yet.

I held my arm close to my side, attempting to ease the jarring of my steps. I gritted my teeth, trying to make sure that Griffin couldn't feel my discomfort. I planned on keeping my promise, but the pain wasn't unbearable...

At least, not yet.

Ten distinct scents hit me when we intersected the route the enemy had taken to reach our friends. I sniffed and tapped into my wolf so I could maintain a decent speed. Soon, Killian's and Sierra's scents mixed with theirs, which wasn't surprising. The enemy had been tracking them after all.

Unlike what I'd told them to do, Killian and Sierra seemed to have run in some sort of random pattern. There were sections where their smells veered off in two different directions. Killian must have been trying to confuse the enemy on where their end goal was by having them run in circles.

The tactic was smart but risky. They were lucky that the others hadn't figured it out and caught them before they got to the cave. But it must have bought them some time, and was probably the reason the fight had just started.

We need to move quietly. The men stalking them would be more focused on what was in front of them instead of behind. They'd expect their friends to have taken us down. *Where's my knife?* I stopped and faced Griffin.

Here, he linked and handed it to me, along with the sheath.

I squatted and fastened the sheath around my ankle, already feeling more like myself. For some reason, this knife always made me feel safer. More grounded. Maybe because it had been my grandfather's. *Okay, we should take out as many as we can without shooting.*

Your shoulder, he growled.

I'll use my left hand. We'd been trained to use weapons with both hands, just in case our dominant side was injured. There'd been so many times I'd thought Dad was being dramatic, but all of those lessons were coming in handy now. *It won't be a problem.*

I wished I could tell my dad I was sorry and that he was right. I'd been so disrespectful at times—rolling my eyes and complaining to Zoe about how stupid it all was. Had I known what our future held, I would've taken it all more seriously.

Pivoting in the direction of the cave, I took off slowly. The sheath rubbed my skin a little more than normal because I was barefoot. Not only had my clothes ripped off my body, but so had my shoes. I was able to move more silently than I would have with the rubber soles of my tennis shoes, but I had to take Griffin's footwear into account as well.

Gunshots kept firing, which brought me peace of mind. If the enemy continued to fire, that meant Killian and Sierra were alive. They hadn't been taken out or hurt yet.

"What's the plan?" a guy asked, from not even a quarter-mile ahead. "They've got coverage, and every time we try to move so they're in view, they shoot. I don't know how the hell we're going to get to them."

Thank God my plan was working. Sometimes, even the most well-thought-out plans went awry.

A row of thick bushes appeared a few feet away, and I got down on my hands and knees and crawled toward them. Griffin moved beside me, following my lead, and soon, we were peeking through the branches.

Two enemies were standing about fifty feet away near a large redwood.

"We have to figure it out," the shorter one said hatefully. "We all have too much on the line if we fail. Besides, we don't need some woman alpha thinking she can rule over us. She needs to be put in her place like any bitch with visions of grandeur should be."

He sealed the deal.

Shorty would be my first target. Maybe I should stand over him all alpha-like as he choked on his own blood.

Okay, I didn't mean that. Even the idea of killing that dickhead turned my stomach, but I would kick his ass.

What's the plan? Griffin lifted his gun, aiming for the one on the right.

The problem was I had a hard time with the concept of killing people who weren't even aware that they were in danger. Call me a glutton for punishment, but it just never felt right. *We'll charge them and try to incapacitate them by hand. If they raise their weapons at us, then we shoot in order to survive.*

I love that you don't want to just kill them, but wouldn't that be the safer solution? Griffin asked as he touched my arm, bringing my attention to him.

Then we'd be the same as them. We couldn't throw our humanity aside and kill because they might attack. What if they didn't? Some of these guys didn't have horrible intentions radiating off them. They might be at the mercy of whoever had leverage over them.

Okay. Griffin sighed. *Let's do it your way.*

Our relationship had changed so much in such a short amount of time. He used to argue and fight with me, and now he was giving in because he could sense my inner turmoil. *Let's go. I'll take Shorty and you take the other guy.*

Rising to my feet, I adjusted my grip on the guns in case we had to fire. I couldn't foolishly pretend these men weren't going to attack. In fact, I knew they would, but I had to see it with my own eyes.

The two of them were so focused in front of them that they didn't see us move until the breeze shifted and blew our scents toward them.

Shorty stiffened and turned, his cold, dark eyes focusing

on me. He hissed, "Stupid bitch. But this makes the job easier for us." He raised his gun, but before he extended his arm completely, a gun fired, and a bullet hit him between the eyes.

"Bo," the other guy hollered, and he charged at me. "You're going to pay for that."

However, he focused his attention on the wrong person. I wasn't the threat.

The next shot fired, and the guy's eyes widened as he realized his mistake. Griffin fired off two shots, each hitting the center of the enemy's torso. He clutched his chest—as if that would stop the blood—then dropped his gun. Tears streaked his cheeks, and he dropped to his knees as the life began to leave his body.

But I couldn't feel bad. They'd forced our hands. We'd tried not to come at them with weapons first thing.

Forcing myself to turn away now that neither of the men was a threat, I raced with Griffin toward the cave. The gunfire had stopped, and fear dug inside me.

Please let them be alive, I chanted internally, over and over again.

The cave came into view, and I scanned the area for threats. All I found was body after body of the enemy, dead on the forest floor. However, I couldn't see Killian and Sierra from my position. All I saw was the dark opening.

"Who's there?" Killian called out. "Don't take another step toward us or you'll force us to shoot." He could hear us but wasn't able to tell who we were.

I counted bodies and realized that, between the two groups we'd killed, all twenty of our enemies were dead. "It's us. They're all gone."

"Sweet Jesus," Sierra gasped. "I didn't think we were going to make it out alive."

That made two of us. "We need to get out of here in case they have backup coming." If their leader didn't hear back from the crow or someone soon, there was no telling how many people they would send next time.

The two of them stepped from the corner of the outside wall of the cave and into view. Neither appeared injured, so that was another miracle that we all had to be thankful for.

"Why didn't you guys go inside?" I asked.

Killian shook his head. "They were firing right at us, and if we ran in, it would've been directly in the line of fire...so, we found a divot in the side where we could shoot from our angle, and they had to come into our line of fire to see us." Killian frowned when his eyes landed on the spot of blood on my shirt. "What happened?"

"I got hit, but it's already healing." I took Griffin's hand and squeezed lovingly. "Griffin removed the bullet—that's why it took us longer to get back to help you."

"You shouldn't have gotten hit in the first place," Griffin grumbled, as his guilt slammed into me.

"It wasn't your fault." There was no way my injury could've been prevented. He and I had done the best we could under the circumstances.

"Come on." Griffin tugged me back toward the house. "You're right. We need to get moving."

If he thought I'd be dropping this conversation, he'd soon learn differently. But getting the hell out of here had to be our number one priority.

"Grab more of their guns." The more we had, the fewer they had. "At least the ones nearby."

"Good idea." Killian bent down and picked up several guns.

Sierra grabbed one and held it awkwardly away from her body.

"Here, give me that." I took it from her. "You're going to get shot like that, which means you need to learn how to shoot when we get back."

"Uh, I'd rather not." She lifted a hand and blew out a breath like she was relieved that I'd taken it from her.

"Unfortunately, you're lumped in with us now, which means you must learn how to protect yourself." There was no room for negotiation. "Now let's go before we have to fight again."

The four of us trekked through the woods, running as fast as we could with our hands full of weapons. When my house came back into view, I had honestly expected to see more vehicles there, but no one new had shown up. Hope ballooned in my heart that we might get out of here without another battle.

"You two need to ride with us," Griffin commanded as he pulled the keys from his pocket and unlocked the car.

"No, I have fix-a-flat. We can be ready to roll in a few minutes." Killian sped up, running faster than I could with my injury. He reached his truck and got out what looked like a metal canister.

Griffin opened the Navigator's passenger door and helped me get settled. My shoulder screamed at the movement of climbing into the tall car. By the time Griffin jumped into the driver's seat, Killian was done with the tire and getting into the truck, Sierra already buckled in on the passenger side.

We peeled out of the driveway, heading to the neighborhood exit, with Killian squealing right behind us. My breathing grew rapid as we sped around the final turn.

When both vehicles turned onto the main road, racing away from my old home, my heart began to settle. That was until my gaze landed on the drawer that sat between my legs. There was no telling what I might find in there, but there was no time like the present. Who knew if we would make it back to Griffin's home?

I inhaled sharply and bent down, resolved to figure out everything I could from the hidden compartment below.

CHAPTER ELEVEN

Griffin placed his hand on my leg, making the buzz of our connection spring to life. "You don't have to look at that now. We just went through hell back there—you can lie back and close your eyes. We'll be home in about fifteen minutes."

Home.

The place we'd left behind had been that to me for eighteen years—but last night, it had felt almost foreign. Maybe because Mom and Dad were missing, and they were what made it home. Or maybe I'd changed so much that I didn't recognize my prior life any longer.

Who knew?

At the end of the day, home was now wherever Griffin and Killian were. The fact that I was so emotionally invested in two people scared me, but what was done couldn't be undone. I loved each man deeply, but for very different reasons. Killian was like a family member I hadn't even known I was missing until I found him. Well, correction... He'd found me floating in the river and on the run for my life.

Griffin... How did I even explain what he was to me? He was the oxygen I craved—needed—and couldn't live without.

"No, I need to." My gut told me that when we got to the house, I'd crash—my eyes were already beginning to droop. And the longer we kept this drawer of secrets, the more likely something could happen to it. These assholes kept coming at us hard, which meant they'd be striking again.

I placed the drawer in my lap and removed the hidden-door compartment. I reached for the small journal and two loose pieces of paper, leaving the photo album for last.

Selecting the brown and yellow stained sheet of paper, I slowly opened the frayed edges. It appeared to be the oldest document of the bunch, so starting there made the most sense.

The letter was handwritten, and I read each word slowly.

Arian,

Things are improving slowly in Shadow City. There is still corruption, but the angels are settling into the new normal. It only took them close to eight hundred years. The loss of our silver wolf protectors is still felt by everyone.

Orion does a fine job guarding us, and no one has gotten in illegally to our city, but Orion's pack doesn't have the extra skills and blessed magic that your pack does. He is raising his son, Killian, to be the next Shadow Ridge alpha, but I hope it doesn't come to that anytime soon.

Just as my father wished, my goal is to reacclimate your pack into our society—but don't worry, your existence will remain a secret until we're in agreement. Even though we are both new alphas, I believe we're destined to meet and make a difference—for the sake of our children. Shadow City was meant to be a safe haven but, instead, has become a place of entrapment.

Together we will right the wrongs of the past.

Sincerely,

Atticus

HOLY SHIT. "I found a letter between our dads."

"Really?" Griffin looked at the paper in my hands. "What does it say?"

I read it to him, and somehow kept a level voice. "That's insane. Your dad even referenced their children." Little did he know that their children were fated mates. I wished we could've seen both of their reactions when that little fact was brought to their attention.

"What else is there?" he asked.

I pulled out the next piece of paper, and as expected, it was another letter from Atticus. This one looked more recent, and the handwriting, more rushed. I read the words out loud.

ARIAN,

The votes have been cast and counted. The gates of Shadow City will open in a week's time. The hope of reuniting with the supernatural races outside of this city has finally come to fruition. Even though people won't be able to move into the city for a while—and even when they do, they'll have to be approved by the council before admittance—we are allowed to have visitors.

I'd love for you to be my first. Your pack identity will be kept secret, but I would love for you to see how much our city has changed and that this place can be a safe haven for the silver wolves once again.

Please come in two weeks and inform the gatekeeper that Atticus has invited you. I will ensure you are ushered straight to me. Let us make this the kind of world our children can be proud of.

Sincerely,

Atticus

"DAD TRIED to keep a level head, but he really dreamed of our pack making a big impact on the wolf community." Griffin smiled sadly, but there was so much pride reflected in his eyes. "He wanted to help the struggling wolf packs and bring harmony to our world. He'd show me maps of the packs that we knew about prior to the border closing and share his plans with me about how he and I, together, were going to visit and help make things right since we'd been closed off for so long."

"I still don't understand why the gates were closed."

Griffin sighed. "There was some sort of political unrest that made the city go into lockdown, but I don't know the details. I hope Mom knows. Dad hadn't gotten around to telling me since it seemed certain we had so much more time."

"Your father sounds like a kind and amazing person." Griffin had never talked to me about his father, and hearing him open up to me warmed my heart.

"Yeah, that was one reason his death shook me so hard." He frowned and inhaled. "We had all these plans, and the thought of doing them alone hurts a lot. Everyone thinks I'm not interested in leading, but it's not that. I want to carry out his plans, but the thought of doing it alone... It was easier to let Dick Harding handle things while I ran off to school and fucked around."

"I know I'm not your dad, and I would never want to replace him...for many reasons." I tried teasing him because I missed seeing his handsome smile. "But I would love to carry out those plans beside you."

"Since the moment we stopped fighting our bond, I've felt like I'm finally ready to be the kind of leader my dad saw in me." He took my hand and squeezed lovingly. "With you by my side, I want to not only follow my dad's plan, but make our own, too."

"That sounds amazing." And it made our current situation piss me off even more. "We have to find whoever is attacking us and kick their ass so we can actually focus on those goals." Although that certainly sounded a whole lot simpler than it would be.

Irritated, I pulled out the journal and flipped to the first page. Dad's familiar squiggly handwriting hurt my heart. For some reason, I'd expected this to be Mom's. But the journal was in his hidden compartment, so, it only made sense that it was his.

I scanned the first few pages, finding nothing earth-shattering. He mentioned that the new alpha of Shadow City had begun sending letters and how he was concerned that, because of his eagerness to connect, others would learn about us.

But the next entry made my breath stop. Dad described the day his brother left the pack.

He'd never mentioned a brother to me. I had an uncle somewhere in this world and had never known about him. The date of the entry was a year before my birth.

Somehow, I'd thought if I learned that I wasn't the last

silver wolf, a part of me would be relieved... I wouldn't be alone. But this news made me feel even more hollow.

A shell of myself.

Not only was I not the last of my kind, but potentially, I had family who were still alive. Family I'd never met and had no way of finding or contacting. The thought made me feel more isolated than ever before.

The onslaught of emotions hovered over me, and I wasn't ready to deal with them, so I flipped several more pages and paused when I saw the date of my birth.

At least, this should be a happy entry, but the very first sentence didn't make sense to me.

The witch who attended my birth to help heal my mother is the same attending my wife to help birth my son and daughter. I'm so thankful for this because birthing an alpha from our pack is hard enough, let alone another child right after. Never has the same witch assisted with two generations of alphas, but because of this unique circumstance, stronger magic is warranted. I only hope that everyone comes out of this healthy and unscathed.

I stopped reading, completely baffled. Was this even my dad's journal or was it someone else's? But the handwriting was unmistakable. Needing for things to make sense, I continued.

Surprising us all, my daughter, Sterlyn, was born first. For the first time in our history, the alpha heir will be a female. If that isn't a sign that change is coming, my son, Cyrus, dying shortly after birth was. The witch tried to revive him with her magic, but she wasn't successful. If it wasn't for our precious little girl, we'd be falling apart right now. Even though the death of our son will always linger, our little girl will pull us through. She's special. We can already feel it.

I had a brother, and my parents never told me. The realization settled over me, making my stomach turn. The feelings I'd been holding off swept over me like a tsunami. Nothing made sense, and I couldn't help but question if I even knew my parents at all.

"What's wrong?" Griffin asked with alarm.

I'd been trying to keep my emotions in check—not wanting to distress him—but I couldn't any longer. Even if I tried pushing them back, it wouldn't work. The force of my reality crashed over me.

My body grew numb, and I felt like I was suffocating from the turmoil coursing through me. The two odd feelings warred with each other as I seemed to drift out of my own body. I dropped the journal and rocked in my seat, wishing the pain of my injury would take over. That pain I could understand—but not whatever was rooting inside me, taking control.

Sterlyn. Griffin almost screamed. *Come back to me.*

His words might've been in another language because I couldn't process them. All I could focus on was this deep, dark void.

My body jarred and a breeze hit my skin, but I still couldn't shake the feelings inside. I was trapped in my own body, and I didn't know how to break free...or if I even wanted to. If I did, I'd have to filter through these raging emotions that were colliding inside me.

COLD WATER PUMMELED MY BODY, forcing me back to the present. I groaned and tried to jerk away, but strong arms had me locked in place. My head rested against a muscular chest, and the scent of myrrh and leather comforted me. I blinked, finding myself in Griffin's arms under the showerhead in his bathroom instead of in the Navigator.

How did I get here? He must have carried me.

The familiar light-gray tile almost seemed too bright in the room.

"That's cold." My teeth chattered. "What the hell are you doing?"

"You went into shock," he rasped, and kissed my fore-head. "You scared the shit out of us. I didn't know what else to do."

"Us?" My mind tried to catch up. It had been only the two of us in the vehicle.

"Yeah, Killian and Sierra are here. We were at a loss about how to snap you out of it, so I told them I would try this. Killian wasn't thrilled about not helping, but no one but me gets to see you in the shower," Griffin growled. "I told them we'd be right out. They're getting cleaned up too."

The reminder that I had a member of my family out there that I didn't know hit me hard, making the emotions that had been held at bay by the shock of the water stream back inside. My eyes burned with tears, and my throat had dried, but I wasn't able to hold them back any longer.

I almost wished I could recede again as I had in the car, but the protective barrier wouldn't lock back in place. Instead, the feelings coursed through me, and a large sob broke free.

"Baby, what's wrong?" Griffin asked, as he gently put my feet on the cold tile floor. "I don't understand...what happened?"

Not able to verbally speak, I used our mate link to fill him in on the information I'd learned. When I was all done, my soul felt fractured. *All this time, Dad didn't tell me anything. It had to be because he didn't think I was strong enough to handle it, and he obviously was right. I feel broken.*

I may not have known him, but I know that's not true. Griffin leaned back and cupped my face in his hands. *You're the strongest person I've ever met. He may have been waiting to tell you everything, thinking you all had more time. No one would expect your pack to be decimated.*

The cold water turned warmer as it ran down my body. His touch comforted me, and I remembered that Dad had told me there were things he needed to share with me in due time. *Maybe, but that doesn't mean that I'm not at the end of my rope.*

Then lean on me. He stepped closer to me. *I'm here to be your rock and your strength. Let me take care of you in a way that you've been able to do for both Killian and me.*

I nearly laughed. *All I've done is put you two in danger. In fact, it would probably be better if you'd never met me.*

That is not true. His words held such conviction and his eyes locked with mine. *Killian and I were going through the motions. We've both been floundering since the loss of our families, then you came along and gave us purpose. He views you as a sister, and you're the love of my life...my soulmate. You've made him happier than he's been in years, and I'm the happiest I've ever been. Without you, I'd never become the man my father envisioned. And now, not only do I want to become that, but I want to be even more for you.*

But... I still couldn't get past everything they'd gone through.

No buts. He kissed me firmly. *You are stuck with us—especially me—and we have your back. The same way you have ours.*

His warm lips ignited something inside of me—a deep, aching need. He was the light in the dark. My life vest in the raging sea. He was my happiness when I almost lost hope.

My sweet scent of arousal floated around us, and a deep growl emanated from his chest.

"You're injured and upset," he said, but his fingers dug into my arm. "Now isn't the time."

"But I need you." I wrapped my arms around his neck, ignoring the pain in my shoulder. This moment was so much more important. "I love you and want to show you how much," I breathed, pushing every ounce of my affection toward him. I didn't want him to doubt my words.

He responded to my kiss, slipping his tongue into my mouth. *I love you too.*

In this moment, there was no doubt about how we felt for each other. He slowly set me on my feet and turned his head, kissing me deeper. His scruff brushed my face, making my body warm even more.

Grabbing the hem of his shirt, which I was still wearing, he stepped back and slowly removed it from my body, paying close attention to my injury. I stood before him, naked now, and my hands rubbed over his bare chest, down toward his jeans. With shaky hands, I unbuttoned them and pushed down his pants and underwear.

Hold on. He released me and yanked his jeans down his legs. The wet material clung to him, and he leaned against the wall, prying them from his body.

For the first time, he didn't look like the confident alpha I'd always known...but all that did was turn me on more. Finally, he pulled free of his pants and threw them outside the glass shower door. *Okay, maybe that was worth it to see that smile.*

One hand caressed my breast as he backed me into the now warm spray. With his other hand, he grabbed a bar of soap and twisted it into a lather. He placed the bar down and gently cleaned my injured arm. The white froth turned pink, and I washed the soap off.

Him caring for me made my heart beat funny, and not able to wait any longer, I jumped up and wrapped my legs around his waist, primed and ready.

"Let me take care of you," he rasped, as he pressed my back to the tile wall. "You need to make sure not to reinjure your arm."

He entered me slowly, making my mind grow fuzzy. I leaned my head against the wall, closing my eyes, enjoying how he overwhelmed my senses.

As he slipped into me, his teeth nicked the sensitive area of my throat where my mate bond mark was located, driving my wolf to howl in pleasure. He nipped and sucked all the way down to my breast.

I bucked against him, making him groan in pleasure.

The two of us moved as one, completely in sync. He sped up his pace as the friction increased between the two of us. I threw my head back, panting as his teeth nipped my breast.

Our feelings intermingled, and I wasn't sure where he began and I ended, but I wouldn't change it for the world. We climaxed together, our pleasure merging and exploding between us.

We stayed still for a moment, lost in each other, when we heard a pounding on the door. Killian's grave voice said, "Get your asses out here *right now*."

My heart dropped. There was no telling what we had to face once we left this room.

CHAPTER TWELVE

Our moment of peace was over, and anxiety wove through me again. The temporary reprieve that only Griffin could provide was gone.

Griffin's arms tensed around me. "What's wrong?" he called.

"We have a visitor." Killian rapped his knuckles on the door. "I put Sterlyn's clothes in your room so she'll have something clean to change into." His footsteps receded, leaving Griffin and me alone again.

"Of course, he couldn't wait until we got out of the shower," Griffin grumbled.

"Well, someone is here." That thought scared me. Who could be here that he didn't want to name drop? "We better get out there."

"Whoever it is can wait a second." He squirted some shampoo into his hands and rubbed his fingers into my hair, working up the bubbles. "You were shot and need a second to get clean. We don't need an infection setting in."

I bit my tongue, not bothering to mention that my wound was already scabbing over. The point was, it didn't matter—he wanted to take care of me, and I did want to get clean. I had dirt in places it shouldn't be, which was fine in wolf form, but not human.

He quickly washed me, and soon we stepped out of the shower. It hadn't taken more than a few minutes for both of us to rinse off since we'd been under the water for a while. After drying off, I stepped onto the cold, gray tile floor and hurried to the bedroom.

Griffin's bedroom was one of my favorite places on earth for two reasons. The first was that his scent was everywhere; that alone calmed me and made me never want to leave. And second, the room felt like him, but also me. It wasn't a standard bachelor room, but wasn't girly, either. It was as if he'd decorated it with me in mind. The walls were a warm blue that reminded me of the ocean, and the furniture was a dark walnut...even the comforter and sheets were a light muted gray, similar to an overcast sky.

The duffel bags holding my clothes were on my side of the bed, which didn't surprise me. Killian would have been able to smell which side held most of my scent. I dug through one bag and pulled out a pair of dark jeans and a maroon shirt, which I purposely chose in case my wound began bleeding again. Even though the spot would be wet, at least it wouldn't visibly stick out like it would on white or a light color.

I put my underwear on first, knowing that—considering where my injury was located—dressing my bottom half would hurt less than my top. Even though I wanted to rush, I forced myself to not go too fast in case I wound up hurting myself worse.

Griffin walked out of the closet and toward me. "Here, let me help you."

He snatched my bra and helped me put it on, followed by the shirt. His help made the process so much easier.

"After our guest leaves," he said with frustration, "we're going to get you situated in here. There's plenty of room in the closet and drawers, and if you need more space, I'll move my stuff around."

"No, I wouldn't want to put you out." This was his room, after all. I didn't want to cause any problems, and him wanting me to stay here was enough for me. "I can make do with whatever you aren't using."

"Put me out?" He grimaced as his nose wrinkled. "This is your bedroom, too. You have as much right to have whatever you want in here as I do."

A huge smile spread across my face, so wide that my cheeks hurt. Hearing him consider this to be our room made my heart happy.

"Wait..." He ran his fingers through my wet hair as he frowned. "You don't think of this place as your home?" Hurt wafted through our bond.

"I just never wanted to force myself on you like that." I hadn't meant to upset him. "Of course, I do, but I didn't want to push things between us too fast."

"You're my fated mate, whom I've claimed and confessed my love to," he growled and kissed me. *I'm yours, which means everything I have is now yours, too. Get it through your head.*

Feet pounded on the floors, and Sierra said, "You better get your butts out here before Rosemary and Killian go at it. They've been staring at each other, lobbing insults back and forth, and I'm not sure I can hold off the impending argument much longer. Unlike him, I'm not afraid of coming in there—Sterlyn doesn't have any parts I myself don't have."

"Uh...but I do." Griffin released me and winked.

"I'm not so sure," she said. "You've always been kind of wussy."

His mouth dropped open, and he marched to the door and yanked it open. "You don't think I have a penis?"

"No, I do, but it got you to open the door." Sierra gloated as she sashayed into the room and looped her arm through mine on my uninjured side. "Which was the whole point. I figured you two were dressed by now." She tugged me toward the door. "Please get out here because Killian is irritable and worried about you. You scared us all."

"What?" I hadn't done anything. "How?"

"The little freak-out state you were in." Sierra sighed as she leaned toward me. "Killian didn't think Griffin's shower plan would work, but obviously it did. I told him no one would know better than the person's mate."

"For a second, I thought he was going to try to join us," Griffin said protectively. "And that would've caused some problems. But he was wise enough to not follow me into the bathroom with you."

"Oh, he thought about it." Sierra laughed as we entered the den. "But he knew you'd kick his ass out of the house."

Killian was pacing in between the two couches in the center of the living room but stopped when we entered. His dark eyes focused on me and his shoulders relaxed. "Thank God you're back to normal."

I wasn't sure if *normal* was the right word, but I was in a better state of mind than I had been twenty minutes ago. "Let's not push it."

"What the hell happened? They refused to tell me anything," Rosemary bristled, crossing her legs as she angled her knees toward me on the large pearl-gray couch. "Griffin texted me, asking me to come, and then I got the silent treatment when I got here."

"Wait." I turned toward Griffin. "You asked her to come? *Again?*" That surprised me. The two of them didn't like each other very much.

"She can heal people, and you weren't yourself." He shrugged as he sat on a matching loveseat perpendicular to Rosemary. "I asked her to come in case the shower didn't work. Besides, we need an update on Carter, and I don't trust hearing it from him."

"He's a good guy." Killian crossed his arms as his jaw ticked. He looked an inch from having a meltdown of his own.

"Well, thank you for coming so quickly." She'd already helped us more than I'd ever expected anyone to. "And I'm sorry that they didn't fill you in. They should've." I scowled at Killian.

"I was a little preoccupied with worry over you," Killian said as he tugged me away from Sierra and hugged me. "What happened? I haven't been scared like that in such a long time. You took at least ten years off my lifespan."

"Oh, stop." I wrapped my good arm around him while keeping my injured one close. When he squeezed me, I hurt a little, but I wasn't going to complain. "You're healthy as a horse. Nothing could shave off those years."

"This is sweet and all, but why don't you fill me in on what's going on?" Rosemary motioned for me to come to her. "And if you want me to heal your injury, I can."

Under normal circumstances, I'd have said no; I didn't like taking shortcuts. But we could be facing some sort of fight again by tonight, so getting back to full strength would be smart. I pulled away from Killian and faced her. "Are you sure you don't mind?"

"I wouldn't have offered if I did." She arched a brow and

leaned against the back of the couch. "I took you as someone who would know that."

And there was the directness that I admired so much about her. "You're right." I sat next to her, turning my body in her direction.

She waved her hand at my shoulder. "Where exactly is it?"

I moved the collar of my shirt until it showed the dark scabs that covered the wound. They were dark red because of how deep the wound had been.

"You two get shot more than anyone I know." She placed her hand on it, and her hand began to glow.

A warmth soaked into the injury, easing the pain. The healing was coming from the inside out, and within seconds, my shoulder felt normal again. "Thank you." I rotated the joint, enjoying the movement without pain. "That feels so much better."

"No problem." She dropped her hand and pointed at me. "So, obviously there was a fight. Spill."

I sat back and told her everything, wrapping up with the little bit I'd learned in the car. At this point, she deserved to know just as much as Killian and Sierra. Everyone here had sacrificed in more ways than one for me.

"Wow, you had a twin brother and an uncle you knew nothing about." Sierra shook her head and plopped into the seat next to me. She laid her head on my shoulder. "That sucks. I'm so sorry."

"I don't get why you mortals apologize for things that aren't your fault." Rosemary pursed her lips. "Like your insincere apology would make a difference in how a person feels. You didn't do anything wrong, so why would you even fathom saying it? That would be like me apologizing for your darker-blonde hair."

"Wait." Sierra tilted her head and glared at the angel. "What's wrong with my hair?"

Oh, wow. That had regressed quickly. "There's nothing wrong with it."

"They call it dirty blonde for a reason." Rosemary threw both hands up. "That should tell you something, but it's not my fault. It just sucks for you."

"It's *sandy* blonde." Sierra huffed and crossed her arms. "Not dirty blonde."

"That's what all dirty blondes say." Rosemary shook her head. "Call it whatever you want, but it doesn't change facts."

"Dude, I think they might have a catfight over this," Killian whispered, as if no one but Griffin could hear him. "This could get kind of hot."

"Maybe I would've thought that at one time." Griffin's gaze landed on me. "But there's only one girl here who makes me feel that way, and it's neither one of them."

If I hadn't had an out-of-body experience earlier when I was overwhelmed with grief, I'd think I was having one now. The craziness going on around me didn't make any sense, but at the same time, it was comforting. Things almost felt normal.

Girls argued over stupid stuff, and guys wanted to fantasize about a catfight.

"Where is this mysterious uncle of yours?" Rosemary asked, coming back to business.

That was a good question. "I have no clue. He left, and there was no hint about where he might've gone. Maybe when things settle down, I can try to find him." It'd be nice to have him now, but I could focus on only one major thing at a time. "So what happened with Carter? You haven't filled us in yet."

"I swear I don't know how that guy isn't an omega." Rosemary groaned dramatically. "He screamed the entire way back, begging me not to drop him, saying that he was sorry. He clutched on to me so hard he ripped my shirt."

"There're a couple of wolves weaker than him." Killian winced and leaned against the wall. "But not by much."

"That's one reason they targeted him." Rosemary rubbed her temples. "They target people who are easily intimidated or have a lot to lose. There's no telling who might be next."

"But they will contact Carter again." They already had leverage over him. They didn't have to risk being exposed by kidnapping someone else. "I'll need to go back to work and pretend I don't suspect a thing."

"Which means people will know we're back." Griffin sighed. "Not to mention you being bait."

"We've already gone over that." There was no getting around it. This was our best plan.

"Everyone already knows you're back." Rosemary twirled a finger. "The guards positioned outside the house were talking about you pulling in like a bat out of hell. If you wanted to stay under the radar, you should've taken that into consideration."

"Sterlyn was unresponsive." Griffin crossed his arms defensively. "I didn't know what was wrong. I panicked, but once we got settled, I did inform them that everything was okay."

"Tomorrow they'd know, anyway." So what if they'd learned a day early? "It'll be fine."

"Well, it's best if we all stay here," Rosemary said. "That way, if there are any attacks, the five of us are already together."

"You're going to stay with us?" She had her own family and life. "I mean, I'm not complaining, I'm just surprised."

"I told you why." Rosemary's eyes tightened in warning. "And you can't seem to stay out of trouble, so it only makes sense to be close by."

"What are you going to tell your parents?" Griffin blinked in surprise.

"That I'm staying with a friend." She shrugged. "I mean, I consider Sterlyn that anyway, so it wouldn't be a lie. The city is a little tense right now anyway, so it'd probably be a blessing that I was out of their hair regardless."

Wow. She thought we were friends. I liked her, so I'd roll with it. "And we have three extra bedrooms."

Griffin beamed at my words. *That's right.* We *do.*

"You said five." Killian pushed off the wall. "Sierra doesn't need to be wrangled into this. She already survived an attack."

"They might not realize who she is yet." Rosemary glanced at the blonde shifter. "If she goes back home though, they might locate her family, and she could put them at risk."

I hadn't even considered that. Killian should've thought about that before bringing her with him.

"It's fine," Sierra reassured everyone. "It makes sense for me to stay. I want to help you all. It's just a benefit that I could be protecting my family by doing it."

Griffin's phone dinged. He looked at it and groaned. "It's Dick. He's pulling into the neighborhood."

"Then that's my cue to run home and grab some clothes." Rosemary stood and headed toward the back door. "I don't want him to see me here—it'll raise too many questions. Text me when he's gone." She exited the house, and I watched as she took flight.

The fact that an angel was hanging out with us shouldn't raise questions. We were all supernaturals and should be friendly. Maybe that could be part of the plan Griffin and I worked on together.

"What does he want?" Killian asked.

"He said we need to talk. That it's important and involves Luna." Griffin complained.

My heart dropped. What had the bitch done now?

CHAPTER THIRTEEN

"**W**hat do we do?" Sierra stood and rubbed her arms. "I'd rather not run into Dick if I can help it. He hollers at me enough at the bar, and I called out sick because of the whole Sterlyn thing."

"Go into one of the guest bedrooms." Griffin pointed at one of the doors back down the hallway. "I'll meet him outside and try to keep him from coming in."

"I don't care if he knows I'm here," Killian scoffed, and took Rosemary's spot on the couch. "*Dove* can stay in here with me while you take care of business."

"No, she's going outside with me." Griffin shook his head and took my hand. "She's my mate, and we've claimed each other. We need to be seen as a united front."

"Are you sure?" Sierra furrowed her brows. "From what I'd heard, your mom didn't rule by your dad's side, or at least, that's the perception we had on the ridge."

"That's true...but unlike my dad, I have the strongest wolf by my side, and one who can lead in her own right." Griffin kissed my cheek. "And we will not be seen as alpha and alpha mate, but as their leaders together." He stilled. *If you're okay with that.*

The fact that he wanted me beside him in all ways somehow deepened my affection for him. This was more than a mate-ship—it was a true recognition of the alpha wolf in both of us. A weak man couldn't handle a strong woman beside him, but Griffin was anything but that. *More than okay.* I kissed his lips, letting him feel how much that meant to me.

"Yeah. On that note..." Sierra walked out of the room, pretending to dry heave.

"Thanks." Killian groaned. "You're leaving me alone in here and making me watch those two like a creeper."

"If the shoe fits," I teased and gave Griffin a huge kiss, making loud noises.

Griffin's shoulders shook as he wrapped his arms around my waist.

"My eyes!" Killian cried and grabbed a couch pillow, putting it over his head.

A knock at the door turned our moment of fun into thick tension.

Dick was here—and I didn't mean the one that had given me a good time in the shower.

Come on. Griffin intertwined our fingers. *Let's get out there before he gets pissy. He hates waiting.*

A little bit of anxiety flowed into me, alerting me that he was trying to hold the emotion back. That didn't make sense. Why would he feel that way, talking to this man? Griffin was the alpha, not the other way around.

Another round of knocking happened even though we were almost at the door. The asshole could smell us through the door at this point, but he was still being impatient.

What the hell was wrong with this guy? I'd met him for

only a few minutes at the bar right after I'd been attacked on my first day here, and something had felt off about him—but it had to be more than just *off* given the way he was acting, and the emotions churning inside Griffin.

Unable to stop myself, I yanked open the door and stepped outside right into Dick's space, forcing him to take a step back.

His strong, musky sandalwood scent overwhelmed my nose. His short salt and pepper hair was gelled to the point of looking greasy, and he was rubbing his fingers along his dark beard. The suit he wore was the same color as his ebony eyes, and matched the vileness that radiated from inside him.

The bear shifter's attack had thrown me off-kilter. This man had something worse than Luna did stirring inside him. No wonder Luna struggled. She must have inherited it from him.

"What are you doing here?" Dick bit out, before smoothing his face into a charming smile. "Shouldn't you be with Killian?"

"Why would you ask such a thing?" I batted my eyelashes and asked lightly. If he wanted to play games, I could keep up.

"Aren't you dating him?" He chuckled, but annoyance flashed in his eyes. "I wouldn't want you to cause problems between him and Griffin. Killian will take over as alpha of Shadow Ridge's guards one day...surely...so it wouldn't be in Shadow City's best interest for him and Griffin to be at odds —especially over a girl." He reached through the door and patted Griffin's arm.

Wow, I had to admit he was good. He came off like the concerned father type.

"I'm sure you can smell that she's not his any longer,"

Griffin said stiffly at the suggestion of me being with Killian. "So you have nothing to worry about."

"That's what I was afraid you were going to say," Dick replied as he glanced at me, before focusing back on Griffin. "Can we talk?"

Griffin lifted his chin. "Anything you have to say can be said in front of my mate."

"Look, I understand what you think you feel, but I think it's best if we speak alone." Dick cleared his throat, pulling at his tie. "Maybe she can go back in the house or something. Or, better yet—go to Killian's."

The asshole was dismissing me. Yeah, that wasn't going to happen. "No, I think I'm good here...and don't worry." I couldn't help but try to fracture his façade. "Killian is in the house, watching a movie, so he's close by."

"Oh, so he knows about this." Dick's shoulders tensed, but he sighed like he was relieved. "Well, at least that's something."

"Yeah, it is." Griffin wrapped an arm around me and led me to a round, black-wire table and chairs stationed on one side of his concrete front porch. We sat down, facing the front yard, the white siding behind us. Some sycamores were positioned in front for privacy and to provide shade.

"Okay, if this is how this conversation will go." A vein twitched between Dick's eyebrows as he strolled over to us. Other than that slight sign of annoyance, he appeared calm —but there was a storm brewing inside him.

"What's so important that you felt the need to leave Shadow City and drop in on *our* home?" Griffin asked, as he took my hand and laid it on the table in view of Dick.

Dick sat at the edge of his chair with his back completely straight. "Maybe you two are moving a little too fast...and she hasn't been officially introduced to the council yet to solidify things, so I thought I should tell you that I'm worried about you, Griffin."

"Why are you worried about me?" Griffin asked as he looked at me with adoration. "This is the happiest I've been in a long time—maybe ever."

"How much do you actually know about this girl?" Dick leaned forward, waving a hand at me, but still somehow pretending I wasn't even there. His eyes stayed locked with Griffin's as if they were the only two people at the table. "Don't you find it funny that she appears from nowhere, starts dating Killian, and then somehow puts the alpha of Shadow City under her spell? She's climbing the ladder."

Yeah...no. Him not acknowledging me ended now. I refused to be dismissed and treated like I wasn't an equal. "*She* is right here and finds your accusations offensive and boundless."

I'm sorry about this. Griffin linked, stroking my hand with his thumb. *I'm not sure what's gotten into him. He's not normally like this.*

In other words, Dick was normally better at keeping his charade in place. *You have nothing to apologize for.* Now I sounded like Rosemary...but it was true.

"I'm sure you do." He rolled his eyes and rubbed his hands together. "Griffin, I think of you as a son, and I'm concerned. This is a conversation that Atticus would have had with you right now. You and Luna have been friends since childhood, and she loves you—"

"There was never a me and Luna," Griffin interrupted, speaking slowly. "I know that you and Saga—" *That's his mate,* Griffin linked to me, "—hoped that she and I would wind up together, and I stupidly didn't discourage either of you. That's my fault, but it ends now. Dove is my fated mate, and we've claimed each other. Everything is final, and you need to let this go."

"Sometimes lust can be confused for a fated mate connection." Dick lifted a hand as he shook his head, playing the concerned father role perfectly. "You wouldn't be the first who was confused, and Luna is willing to forgive—"

"Are you saying that Griffin doesn't know the difference between lust and a fated mate bond?" I growled as my wolf howled inside; Dick even insinuating that Griffin should be with someone else enraged me.

He must be acting like this because Luna is upset, Griffin justified.

Whether Griffin realized it or not, this prick was insulting his intelligence. I might not have worldly knowledge, but that didn't give Dick the right to disrespect or disregard me. There was no doubt that Griffin and I were fated mates. The feelings were similar—attraction-wise—but lust didn't explain the immediate connection and love that you felt for the person; the acknowledgment of both halves of the same soul seeing each other for the first time.

Dick glared, and the vein somehow appeared larger. "I'm saying that attraction can be a confusing thing and that he wouldn't be the first that thought with his—"

"Dick?" I couldn't stop my mouth from running. "It's funny and fitting that it so happens to be your name."

Babe. Griffin sounded both horrified and amused, which was an odd combination. *I love your sense of humor, but he has been good to me. He's helped me so much since Dad died, so let's at least give him a break and not poke fun at his name, please.*

Oh, shit. Griffin had no clue what this man was really like. He was completely buying Dick's act. I had to tread carefully because this could become a problem between us. It wouldn't break us, but I didn't want to force my opinions on him and make him bitter or resentful. I had to get him to see the truth gradually because Griffin trusted Dick.

Of course, he did.

He was letting this man make decisions on his behalf. He wouldn't do that if he didn't trust him. I needed to warn him about his intent, but honestly, this gift was newer to me, so I wanted to make sure I was reading people correctly before throwing around accusations. Prior to coming here, I was almost always around the same people—none of whom had read negatively to me.

Thankfully, he was talking about taking back control.

"Do you think that's the first time I've ever heard that joke?" Dick lost his calm, and his body turned rigid. "It's very unoriginal, which already confirms my suspicions about you." He held out a hand toward Griffin. "Someone like that wouldn't be the fated mate of the strongest alpha of our species."

Wow, he'd laid it on thick. I had to give him props, he wasn't half-assing. "Look, you're right. That was uncalled for...but you came here, insulting not only me as a person, but my bond with Griffin."

"The fact that you're calling it an insult should prove that you don't have his best interests at heart like I do." He placed a hand on his chest and closed his eyes. "If you were his mate, you would appreciate that I'm worried about him."

Okay, that's too far. Griffin's annoyance flared. *I've given him enough leeway.*

Griffin opened his mouth, but I cut him off; I had to call the guy out on his crap if I wanted Griffin to see things for what they really were. "If you didn't come here and essentially call my mate stupid and insult my intentions, maybe

I'd feel differently. To add insult to injury, you tried to pimp your daughter out to him—despite him telling you that he was never interested—and that our bond is final since we claimed one another. To me, that comes across as pushy and manipulative." I smiled sweetly at him, trying to play one of his own hands against him. "I'm sure you appreciate what I'm saying since it's out of concern, much like your words are."

"Now listen here." He locked gazes with me, challenging my wolf. He planned on forcing me to submit to him. "You don't get to come here and talk to me that way."

"Actually, you came here." I held his stare, effortlessly. This guy might be strong, but he was nothing like a silver wolf, or even Griffin. He had an inflated sense of self-worth, which made him more dangerous. But I refused to look away. Griffin said he wanted us to lead together, so that was exactly what I would do. "You're more than welcome to leave." *I hope I'm not making you angry.* I did care about upsetting Griffin.

No, he's being an ass to you, even if it is out of concern for me. Griffin squeezed my hand lovingly. *You need to stand your ground. It's not okay, what he's trying to do. He has to respect not only me and you but our relationship. So do whatever you feel needs to be done.*

That was exactly what I'd hoped he'd say, but I was relieved that we were on the same page. *I love you.*

I love you too.

Sweat sprouted along the top of Dick's lip as his wolf began to struggle against mine.

My wolf growled inside—but not because she was feeling the strain. She was angry. She could feel the darkness in him too and was both annoyed that he'd questioned my and Griffin's bond, but further irritated that he expected us to submit to him. "Are you feeling okay?" I tilted my head while maintaining eye contact. "You seem to be getting overheated."

"I'm fine," he rasped, his words shaking. He had to be on the brink of submitting to me. The fear reflected deep inside.

In my peripheral vision, I saw him reach a hand into his pocket. A few seconds later, his phone made a noise. He pulled it out and glanced at the screen. "Oh, my phone rang." The smell of a lie was nonexistent because he had, in fact, made his phone ring.

He was a clever asshole.

I wanted to call him on it, but I'd pissed him off enough for one day. "Is everything okay?"

Dick ignored me once again and focused on Griffin. He said, "Consider what I said, and maybe call Luna tonight? She's been worried."

"Look, I've let you have your say." Griffin stood and stepped behind my chair, placing his hands on my shoulders. "I've even watched you be disrespectful to my mate, but that ends now. You are like family to me, but Dove is my claimed fated mate. There is no confusion on either of our ends, and Killian is very happy for us. If you insinuate one more time that Dove is not, in fact, my mate, it will cause problems between you and me, which I would hate."

"You're letting a girl..." Dick sputtered, seeming at a loss for words, "come between us? Luna *loves* you—"

A deep, threatening growl emanated from my chest. If he said that bitch's name one more time, I would attack his ass.

"No, you're going to let my mate come between us." Griffin emphasized each word. "Dove is my mate. She will be moving in with me here, and in Shadow City."

Dick took several deep breaths and then nodded slowly. "Fine, I understand." He pulled on his suit jacket. "Do you by chance have that paperwork signed?"

"Oh, yeah." Griffin relaxed. "Let me go grab it. I'll be right back." *You okay staying out here?*

Not really. The guy made me very uncomfortable—but if I ran in after Griffin, I'd look weak. *Yup. I'm good.*

When Griffin entered the house, Dick smirked, "It would be in your best interest to not get involved with certain decisions. Griffin and I have a system that works. I wouldn't want you trying to interfere more than you already have."

The unveiled threat hung between us. "Or what?" My wolf surged forward, ready to fight.

CHAPTER FOURTEEN

I inhaled deeply as I stood, trying to keep my heart from beating too quickly. I didn't want Dick to think he had some sort of power or influence over me—even if he did. Granted, the emotion he inspired was anger, not fear—but egocentric males like him always tried to make themselves feel more powerful.

Even though it wasn't fear, he would pretend that it was.

"Look, I don't know what you're up to, but Griffin will come around." Dick's nostrils flared as he marched over, crowding into me.

He wanted to make me feel threatened and to step back, but I refused to budge. Instead, I lifted my chin and looked down my nose. "Yeah, he will. I agree. He's smarter and stronger than you give him credit for."

A frown peeked from the corners of his mouth, and he inhaled sharply, making his chest touch mine.

Even though he had multiple layers on, and I was wearing a thick shirt, I still felt dirty. An ickiness coated my skin, and my natural inclination to jerk away almost took over.

Almost.

But I used every ounce of self-control I had to prevent that. He was doing anything possible to force me to be the one to cower first, and I couldn't let the asshole win—even though my desire to jerk away had nothing to do with me actually wanting to submit to him, but rather to get away from the maliciousness that wafted from him and coated me.

Griffin's footsteps grew louder as he approached the front door once again.

Unfortunately, Dick was smart enough to take a step back, an amicable smile replacing the scowl from moments before. He was going back to his little persona that worked on my mate. But it wouldn't last for long.

I'd make sure of it.

The front door opened, and there was Griffin with a stack of papers in his hands.

I wanted to ask what they were, but it didn't matter—I could see his signature on the back few pages, so I could only hope that he'd read the documents thoroughly before signing.

"Thank you," Dick said as he swiped them from Griffin's hand. "I should be getting back to Shadow City now so we can file these with the council."

"Very well," Griffin said as he nodded, and placed an arm around my waist. "And I understand that Luna may be upset, but she'll be okay. Don't worry. With time—and when she finds her fated mate—things will get better."

"Not everyone finds their fated mate." Dick cut his eyes over at me. "You know that."

He must have thought that if he kept insinuating we

weren't fated mates, Griffin would believe him. The arrogance behind the strategy was insane. Even if we weren't fated mates, we'd claimed each other. Our bond was complete, and the only thing that could break it was...

Death.

My heart sank.

Could that be his plan?

"But that was before we began leaving the city and integrating back into the world." Griffin kissed my cheek and continued, "If we hadn't done that, then I would've never found St—Dove." *Shit, I'm sorry. It's just...Sterlyn fits you so much better.*

Dick's eyebrows rose, but what made me most nervous was that he didn't comment. That meant he'd noticed Griffin's near slip and stored the information.

I cringed. The less Dick learned about me, the safer we all were. At least Griffin had caught his slip before my whole name came out. *It's okay. Just got to be more careful.*

"Well, then. I guess I better go." Even though Dick's face was smooth, there was a slight edge to his voice. "I'll see you soon." He turned around and strolled toward the black Mercedes.

That was when I noticed there was someone in the driver's seat—like a chauffeur.

Who the hell did this guy think he was? The president or something? *Why does he have a driver?*

No clue. Griffin chuckled. *He's had one for as long as I can remember.*

But you don't? You'd think out of the two of them, Griffin would be the one with that kind of luxury. I understood that the guy was on the council, but Griffin was the alpha heir.

God, no, he replied as we watched Dick's car pull out

and drive away. *I like being behind the wheel. Dad was the same way, but from what I understood from Dad, Dick's whole family is like that.*

Dick had to be who my dad had sensed was still corrupt. The amount of negativity coming off him was enough to upset my stomach. There was a little badass in everyone, but I'd never encountered something that awful before. Even the people attacking us weren't that negative— though, granted, we'd learned that some of them weren't doing it willingly.

Griffin opened the door, and I entered, brushing past him.

Killian remained on the couch, watching television. He paused the show. "So, what'd he want?"

Oh, this would be all me. "To inform Griffin that he thinks our fated mate bond is only lust and that Griffin belongs with Luna."

"Wow." Killian pursed his lips. "Took a long time for him to say those two things."

"He was long-winded." Griffin plopped onto the loveseat and patted the space beside him. "But don't worry, Sterlyn put him in his place and had a semi-standoff with him."

"That he ended." At least the dumbass was smart enough to know when he couldn't win. "Sierra, it's safe to come out now."

The bedroom door opened, and she padded down the hallway toward us. "That didn't take as long as I was afraid it would. Did he catch my scent?"

"He didn't say anything." That was the one good thing about the entire situation. "He was too preoccupied trying to get Griffin to leave me for *Luna.*" It angered me that I even had to say her name in the same sentence as my mate's.

"And I always thought he was smart." Sierra shook her head. "But everyone can smell your scent on each other. He knows that you're both claimed."

"Oh, he knew." I tried to pretend like I wasn't watching Griffin's reaction. "And he mentioned how I'd better not get involved with any council or city decisions."

"What?" Griffin's face tensed as his jaw twitched. "Where was I?"

"Where do you think, dumbass?" Killian deadpanned and crossed his arms. "In here getting whatever paperwork he had drawn up for you to sign."

"Speaking of that." I had to ask. There was no way I couldn't, especially now that Killian had brought it up. "Please tell me you read over the documents before signing."

"Of course, I did. It's authorization for some of the Shadow City guards to get more training." Griffin waved off the concern as he turned his body toward me. "But he threatened you, and you didn't use our link to tell me?"

"It wasn't a big deal." Right now, Dick was the least of my concerns. Well, that was an exaggeration, but considering how few people could actually leave the city, I doubted that my attackers were Shadow City residents. "I can handle him. Dad prepared me to handle sexist wolves my entire life."

"Really?" Sierra sat on the other end of the couch from Killian, closest to me. "He's kind of over the top. At work, he pretends that I don't exist unless he has to talk to me. Of course, it's usually to tell me to go clean the bathrooms or some other sort of 'woman's work.'"

Griffin's brows furrowed. "That's surprising. He never treats the women on the council that way."

"That's because they aren't wolves, and he needs something from them, man." Killian leaned back and placed his hands behind his head. His arms flexed, revealing how muscular he was. "Have you not noticed this before now?"

"No." Griffin ran a hand through his hair. "But it kind of makes sense. We were locked away, and our culture is archaic because of that."

"Shadow City isn't the only place like that." I'd been prepped and warned. "Dad told me I'd experience that kind of sexism in the world, and honestly, there was some even in my own pack. But it doesn't matter because, at the end of the day, I'm stronger than Dick, and there is absolutely nothing he can do about that."

"Girl, I knew I liked you from the get-go." Sierra leaned over the end of the couch and patted my arm. "Change is coming, and poor ol' Dick will wind up a limp noodle before it's all done."

"What?" Killian's face smooshed in disgust. "Really? You two are like sisters to me, and you're making sexual innuendos in front of me?"

"Would you rather we act them out?" Sierra gave me a huge smile, revealing both rows of her teeth.

"Maybe bringing you here was a bad idea." Killian pouted and bounced a leg. "Between your comments and Griffin pawing at Sterlyn, I'm going to have nightmares." He pointed at me. "What happened to keeping your legs closed nice and tight?"

Laughter spilled out of me, and I hadn't realized how much I needed the release. During the first week I'd stayed with Killian under the ruse of dating him, he'd found out I was a virgin and been shocked. I'd made that comment to explain things to him.

"Oh, don't worry." Griffin wrapped an arm around my shoulders, pulling me into his side. "She still does for everyone else but me."

Killian huffed and stared at the television like he was too disgusted to look at any of us.

"Well played," Sierra said, as she saluted Griffin. "He's speechless for once."

Comforting warmth expanded in my chest. In this moment, things felt normal; four friends hanging out, trying to get a reaction from one another. In fact, I'd never gotten to experience things like this until I found Killian and Griffin. They'd given me a piece of normalcy that I hadn't been able to find with my birth pack—a sense of belonging that let me know that life might be shitty, but there were bright spots.

Spots that I cherished more because of the bad.

Not that I wouldn't love to have my parents here with me, along with the brother I'd never gotten to meet. I would —so damn much—but that wasn't possible, no matter how much I wished it.

There's a sense of happiness ebbing from you. Griffin intertwined our fingers. *I've never felt this from you before.*

Is that a problem? I teased, able to feel how pleased he was. *Should I be broodier?*

God, no. He tucked a piece of my hair behind my ear. *I hope you feel like this more often. You look even more breathtaking right now.*

"Ew," Sierra groaned. "Maybe I was wrong to give you hell. It is kind of sickening to watch them be all lovey-dovey."

"Nope, you sided with them." Killian crossed his arms and bared his teeth. "You don't get to complain. That right is solely reserved for me."

The flapping of wings notified us that Rosemary had returned. The back door swung open, and her rose scent swirled into the room as she stepped inside with a black duffel bag slung over her shoulder.

"Well, come on in." Sierra snorted. "Make yourself at home."

"I believe I just did." Rosemary strolled to us. "Which bedroom am I staying in?"

As usual, we could count on her to get straight to the point.

"The bedroom down that hallway on the right." Griffin gestured in the same direction that Sierra had come from. "You'll be on the other side of the hall from Sierra's and Killian's rooms. Sterlyn and my room are at the very end of the hallway."

"Good, I'll be close to Sterlyn." Rosemary frowned and gestured to me. "If someone attacks, I'll be her best ally."

"Uh...I'm the alpha of the protectors of Shadow City." Killian pounded on his chest. "If anyone—"

"You and your pack are the protectors by default." Rosemary flipped her hair over her shoulder. "And only because angels have more important jobs than watching for potential threats. We come to your aid in wars, but Sterlyn's pack was always meant to be the true protectors."

Killian growled.

She'd kind of insulted me and praised me in the same breath, and made Killian feel inferior. "We need to work on your manners."

Are you sure that's wise? Griffin asked.

I trusted my gut. *We'll find out.*

"Excuse me?" She frowned, her twilight eyes blazing. "I'm only speaking the truth."

"Being rude and speaking the truth are two different things." That was part of the problem—no one ever tried to explain to her why what she said was uncalled for. If no one was going to correct her, I would. "Killian and his pack have sacrificed a lot to protect Shadow City and their own. To the point of losing his entire family. Do you think calling him weak and telling him he does something you find worthless is the way to make him want to help protect you?"

"It's not worthless." Her face fell. "I just meant that angels—"

"Stop." I stood and placed a hand on her shoulder. "Angels have other things they are responsible for, but they don't mind coming to help fight when an adversary rises."

"That's what I said." She blinked and looked at the others.

"No, it was most definitely not." Sierra pinched the bridge of her nose. "You said that angels have more important jobs."

"Which is—" Rosemary started, but I raised a hand.

"Not true." I leveled my gaze at her. "You don't think protecting Shadow City is an important job even though Killian's pack aren't silver wolves?"

"Oh." She bit her bottom lip as realization dawned on her. "Yeah, okay. I see what you're saying." She pivoted toward Killian and frowned. "I'm sorry. I didn't mean it like that. Sterlyn is right—the way I worded things was inconsiderate. It's just—"

"That's good." I had a feeling if she kept going, it would negate everything she'd just said; I was surprised that she'd apologized on her own. "That was very nice of you. Wasn't it, Killian?" I glared at him, daring him to not cooperate.

"To say I was shocked would be an understatement," Killian offered.

"All you all have to do is point things out like Sterlyn does." Rosemary blew out a breath. "If something bothers you, just say it. That's what's wrong—"

"Let's get you situated." I grabbed her hand and pulled her toward the bedroom Griffin had pointed to. "And then we all need time to relax before tomorrow." And I meant that, even if we relaxed separately.

I YAWNED as Griffin and I walked into the coffee shop on the Shadow Ridge University campus extra early the next morning. The night before hadn't been as relaxing as I'd hoped because Rosemary had watched a movie with us. I'd been on edge, waiting for her to make Killian or Sierra angry again. She hadn't, and the night had been pleasant, but the anticipation had kept me a little tense.

The inside of Shadow Ridge Coffee looked like a standard coffee shop. A few tables were scattered around the room, and two espresso machines were positioned in the center of the counter, with the cash register on the right.

Carter walked out from the back, and his face fell when he found the two of us there. I snatched an apron from the hook on the wall behind the counter, refusing to let his reaction bother me. Of course, my return made him tense because whoever had ordered him to drug me was probably watching.

"It's so good to have you back." Carter tried to sound sincere, but the sulfuric stench of a lie wafted around us.

"Just act normal," Griffin growled, lowly. "Or you're going to get us all killed." *Maybe this wasn't a smart idea after all.*

We got here early so you could hang out and get comfortable before your classes. I kissed him and then went to the cash register. *We have to act normal if we want this to work.*

"God, remember no PDA here." Carter stomped a little

and grabbed some of the items needed for the espresso machine. "And I thought you and Killian were bad."

A loud rumble bellowed from Griffin.

Great, this day was starting out wonderfully.

"Right, Killian did kiss her often." Luna's voice rang in my ears. "I wonder what else they might have done in here when no one was looking."

And there she was. I'd figured she and I would have it out soon. No better time than the present.

CHAPTER FIFTEEN

The insinuation that Killian and I might have had sex had Griffin visibly shaking beside me. I touched his arm, trying to calm him. *You know that's not even remotely true.*

Luna sashayed to the cash register and flipped her golden bronze hair over her shoulder. Her Caribbean blue eyes landed on my hand, and she straightened her back, probably trying to appear as tall as possible despite being two inches shorter than me. She smirked and said, "I wonder where you've touched Killian prior to you and Griffin getting together."

That bitch wanted to cause problems, but little did she know that my relationship with Killian hadn't been like that. We'd been exclusive, but only to prevent her from trying to hook Killian up with her best friend. Griffin was fully aware, so the only person he was getting angry with was her. "For someone who has so much interest in Griffin, you're very focused on Killian's and my *former* relationship."

"Well, I just want to make sure that Griffin has fully thought through the implications of being with you." She lowered her head and pushed out her breasts so the cleavage framed by her skimpy, thin, royal-blue sweater's low neckline was available for view. It was a miracle her nipples didn't pop out.

I swear, if she doesn't shut up— Griffin was so enraged that he couldn't finish the sentence.

"He has, just like he thought out *not* wanting to be with you." My skin tingled as my wolf got riled too. If I wasn't careful, I'd shift, and we didn't need Luna knowing more about me than she already did.

"It's funny." She crossed her arms, lifting her boobs even more. "You're doing a whole lot of talking, and he's remaining quiet."

"Luna, we're not open yet." Carter hurried over and wiped sweat from his brow. "Why don't you come back in ten minutes when everything is open and ready?"

She didn't even acknowledge the poor guy and took a few steps closer to Griffin. She pouted and lowered her voice as she reached for him. "It's not too late—"

Griffin stepped back out of reach and glared. "Do *not* touch me. In fact, don't come near me or Dove ever again."

"Are you fucking serious?" She dropped her hand and sneered. Unlike her dad, she didn't have a good poker face— but maybe that would improve the longer she practiced. "She's an outsider who screwed your best friend, and you want her instead of me?"

"He not only wants me...he *chose* me." I was going to make this crystal clear. If I had to pee on Griffin's leg, so be it. I pointed at the faint teeth-mark scar on my neck. "The decision has been made, and Killian has given his blessing, so why don't you leave like Carter asked, and maybe don't bother coming back."

Her mouth dropped open, and her breathing increased. "Tell me this is some kind of joke." She looked at Griffin. "This can't be real."

"It is real, and you need to get it through your head that you and I will never be together." Griffin walked behind the counter and wrapped an arm around my waist. "I never wanted you, and you knew it. The only reason I became your friend in the first place and tolerated your grand delusions was because of your father; I didn't want tension between him and me. But I was being a coward."

"That's not true." She huffed, not noticing the trickle of people entering the coffee shop now that we were open.

Carter groaned as if realizing that, once again, I was causing a scene. In a way, he should have been thankful. I'd bet that my employment here was helping business because people wanted to come by in case something else happened. I probably should get a raise.

"We kissed that one—" she started, and a low threatening growl escaped me.

The fact that his lips had been on hers rattled not only me, but my wolf as well. *You kissed her?* I didn't have a right to be angry. The instance obviously occurred before we committed to each other—but the thought of his lips on anyone else's made me see red.

She smirked, thrilled with my reaction.

"Don't change the story," he snarled. *It wasn't like that, at all.* His fingers dug into my waist a little as his anger increased. "You got me drunk and kissed me, trying to do more. Even in my drunken state, I pushed you off me."

"That's not true." But the sulfuric smell of a lie wafted around us.

A few of the shifters who had walked in coughed at the rancid smell.

Her body stiffened, and she glanced over her shoulder, seeming to realize that we had an audience. She must have been so caught up in her anger that she hadn't noticed when they'd entered.

"Look, it's obvious that he's never been into you." I was so tired of people not telling the truth; people needed to be direct. Like Rosemary. The angels had that right. It was something we shifters should embrace too. "Ever. It's not my fault, even if you can't see it that way."

"He's confused." Luna spread her arms out. "That's all. It makes better sense for him to be with me. I'm going to be part of the council in the future—taking over my father's spot. I know how things work in the city. I decided to come to college to get the best education so I can be valuable in the future."

I'm going to follow your lead. Griffin waved his hand in front of his chest. "Maybe that's all true. But you didn't make those plans until I decided to come here."

Okay, he had laid it out there for her. Sugarcoating only got you so far.

"Griffin..." She stomped a foot, reminding me of a child. "Don't do this. We're good for each other."

"Listen, I'm not sure how much clearer I can make this for you." Surely if I ticked off everything on the list, the truth would finally click. Something had to work or Griffin and I might hurt her. And even though I didn't like Dick, we had to be strategic—hurting his daughter was not part of a good strategy.

I lifted one finger. "He's claimed me." With each point, I lifted another one. "I've moved in with him. He's never been interested in you, and you're coming off pretty pathetic right now."

"You're such a bitch." She leaned across the counter, getting into my face. The corruption emanating from inside her seemed to darken to nearly the same shade as her father's. "You will learn your place sooner or later."

"Or maybe you'll be the one who actually figures it out." One of the first alpha lessons Dad had taught me was when I started elementary school. Another shifter there didn't like me immediately; some boy who was the alpha heir of his father's pack. He could sense my strong wolf, and because of our animal nature, he tried to assert his dominance. Dad told me that standing down from a bully, especially a supernatural one, only encouraged future mistreatment. I hadn't believed Dad at first, but each day, the bullying grew worse until I finally made the boy submit to me. He didn't return to school the next day.

This was the same situation—but instead of a boy, it was a girl vying for her sexist father's approval. There was no telling how she'd grown up, and judging by the way Dick had acted at the house yesterday, he was probably the reason that Luna was so desperate to be with Griffin.

But Dick was never going to change, and she probably didn't want to see that. Maybe at one time, I could have felt bad for her, but not now. Not anymore. She was old enough to make her own decisions, and her soul was darkening on her own accord.

"You don't want to mess with me," she threatened, her face turning slightly red from her anger. "You have no clue what I'm capable of."

But that wasn't true. I did. It wafted from her and slammed into me, making me feel gross. "And you don't know anything about me. You may not like me—hell, the feeling is mutual—but I'm Griffin's mate, and I'm not going anywhere." I leaned over, getting even more in her face; she had to realize that I would not be intimidated by her or anyone else.

"I want to add," Griffin rasped, "this is the last time you get a reprieve from talking to my mate like that. If you so much as look at her in a hateful manner, we'll become enemies. I don't give a flying fuck if Dick is your dad. Do I make myself clear?"

Her bottom lip quivered, and she stood up straight. "This isn't over."

"Oh, but it is." I lifted my chin and laid my head on Griffin's shoulder. We had presented a united front, and there wasn't a damn thing she could do about it.

Her irises turned navy before she spun on her heel and marched past the growing line of people and out the door.

"Dove, I swear." Carter sighed and waved to the next person in line. "There is never a dull moment with you around."

"Yeah, I have to agree." I wished that wasn't the case. At some point, things had to calm down...surely.

THE NEXT FEW days flew by. Luckily, Luna didn't come back. She'd left with her tail between her legs—but if she was anything like her father, that wouldn't last long. She'd come back at me, but when Griffin wasn't around.

I counted out the drawer as Griffin entered the shop. He scanned the area like he expected to find Dick or Luna inside.

Stand down, Cujo, I teased. *Only Carter and I are here.*

That does not make me feel any better. He strolled over to me with a frown on his face. *He's the one who injected you with a drug and handed you over to that bear shifter.*

He did have a point. *True, but he's on our side now.*

Supposedly, Griffin growled as Carter walked out of the kitchen and behind the counter.

"Oh, yay." Carter sighed. "Your boyfriend is here while we're closing...like he has been the entire week."

"Mate," Griffin corrected, and kissed me. "And sorry if I don't like her being alone with you."

"I made a mistake." Carter's shoulders sagged.

"Let's not talk about this now." We were supposed to be acting normal, and if anyone was watching closely, our cover was blown. "Carter has been a good friend." Hopefully, that last sentence would throw anyone off if they were somehow listening or keeping an eye out. No one would expect me to call him that if we knew what he'd done.

I closed the till and smiled sweetly at Griffin. "Are you ready to go?" We needed to act upbeat and not worried.

"Yeah, we'll see you later, man." Griffin stood and waved at Carter. He took my hand, and we walked out the door together.

If you keep acting angry with him, he'll be hesitant to help us if they call. Carter might feel like it would anger Griffin more, and we really needed him to be comfortable informing us.

I usually agree with you, but not on this one. Because he knows I'm pissed, he'll call first thing. He kissed my cheek as we entered the hallway between the campus bookstore and cafeteria.

The seating inside, and the picnic tables just outside the

glass back doors, were full. The view out back was beautiful with the scenery of the river and woods. The scents of maple and redwood swirled in the air. Most of the shifters were outside while the vampires were mostly inside.

Maybe he had a point. Carter did seem upset that Killian and Griffin were mad at him. In a way, those two had been angrier than I had been...and I was the one who'd been kidnapped. Granted, if something happened to either one of them, I wouldn't be quick to forgive either.

We turned down the hallway to the front doors. The walls were the standard institutional beige, and the floor a warm, gray tile. A few students passed by us, heading in the opposite direction as we passed by the second hallway, which housed various administrative departments.

Griffin opened the wooden front double doors and waved me through. Of course, the scent of honey vanilla musk overpowered my nose.

The bitch was here...again.

My gaze found Luna sitting on one of the benches in front of the school. Her focus had already been set on us, like she was waiting for us to come outside.

Ignore her, Griffin said, as he angled us so that he walked in front of her like a barrier.

My natural instinct was to move so I was on that side, but he wanted to make a point to her that he would protect me. I couldn't dissuade him even if I wanted to. He wasn't trying to make me look weak—he was showing that he had my back.

She growled faintly as we walked by but didn't say anything, which unnerved me. She liked to run her mouth, and her not doing so made me think she had ulterior motives.

We continued past her and soon climbed into Griffin's Navigator and headed home.

"Should we be nervous that she didn't say anything to us?" I already knew the answer but wanted to hear his take.

"No. She gives me the cold shoulder whenever she's mad at me." He shrugged. "She'll be trying to talk to me again soon enough. Just enjoy the quiet."

He sounded so sure, but the quiet was what scared me. I reached over and took his hand, enjoying the feel of his skin.

———

A FEW DAYS LATER, I found Rosemary in the living room. "How did everything go at the coffee shop?" Rosemary asked, pacing the room like she'd been on edge.

"Luna hasn't come in since the incident," I said as I walked to the loveseat and dropped onto it. "So other than her staying away, nothing out of the ordinary." The girl did like being the center of attention.

Killian walked out of the kitchen and joined us. "Well, Rosemary here has been pacing the room since she got back. Each day, she gets more amped up. She's been a whole lot more nervous about Sterlyn going to the coffee shop than she let on." He took his usual spot on the couch and smiled at the angel.

Wait...he was smiling at Rosemary. What dimension had I entered? They had seemed to be getting along more amicably the past few days, but I hadn't expected them to be friendly.

"If you've been that worried, why didn't you go keep an eye on her?" Griffin asked, angrily.

"Because Carter and I flew off together the morning I brought him to talk to you." Rosemary scowled back at him.

"So if I looked protective and whoever is behind all this was watching, they might become alarmed. We have to be smart."

Killian tensed, somehow adding more tension to the air. He glanced at us and cleared his throat. "Carter just linked me. He said Rosemary needs to meet him. They finally made the call."

CHAPTER SIXTEEN

The ride to Shadow Lake passed in a tense silence. One of Griffin's hands was on the Navigator's steering wheel while the other one gripped my leg like I might disappear. As if his grasp was the only reason I was still sitting beside him.

Killian sat behind my seat, breathing heavily with his own anxiety. "I can't believe I'm coming back here."

"Wait... What do you mean?" Something must have been bothering him more than I realized.

He didn't respond, and Griffin linked with me, *His family died where we're heading.*

Oh, my God. "Killian, you don't have to come—"

"Hell, yes I do," Killian growled. "I'm not having the two people I consider family go here without me. Never again."

I already felt like I was suffocating, and their stress-filled demeanors only increased mine—but there wasn't anything I could do about it. If I reacted, it would cause them to become even more stressed. Besides, to be fair, if one of them were in the same situation, I'd feel the same way. "Okay, but if it gets to be too much—"

They were upset because they cared, and even though I was miserable because of it, I wouldn't change them feeling this way for the world.

Both of them were my family.

"Please stop." Killian exhaled. "I'm going. It'll be fine. We aren't going to hang out—we'll be dealing with shit so I won't have time to think about it."

Griffin glanced in the rearview mirror. "Are you sure he won't fuck this up?"

"Dude, how many times do we have to go through this?" Killian grumbled. "He's meeting Rosemary in the woods behind the pack neighborhood, and he's willingly letting her fly him to Shadow Lake to meet us to ensure he isn't followed. You need to keep your attention on the road and make sure no one is following us."

"Including any damn crows." I still hated that one. I'd been staring out my windshield, paying more attention to the sky than the road behind us. My stalker's first crow was dead, but there was no telling whether he had another that had stepped in.

Wow—he... I might be as sexist as Dick. Why couldn't the bad guy be a girl?

Great, I was losing it. Scolding myself and having internal debates revealed that little nugget.

Griffin smirked. "I'm so glad I shot that bastard."

"That was too kind after everything he'd done." I had wanted to be the one to end him. "I planned to pluck out each feather one by one before providing a slow and painful death."

"Damn, Sterlyn," Killian chuckled. "And here I've been thinking that you were kind and empathetic—only killing when required—but then you spout off something like that."

"I'd planned on killing the bear shifter who attacked

me." I'd been ready to get my revenge. "But when he was lying helpless, crumpled on the ground...I just couldn't do it." To actively kill someone like that in cold blood... I didn't have it in me.

"Hey, I was teasing." Killian placed a hand on my shoulder and rubbed. "I know—when it came down to it—you wouldn't have been able to kill the crow, even though he deserved it."

Maybe not, but...the crow was a little different. He'd put not only me but the people I loved in danger.

"I won't be nearly as kind as her if Carter tries to put one over on us again." Griffin's hand tightened even more.

Hey, everything is going to be okay. If he didn't breathe, he could have a heart attack like his father. "He told us they called; I think we're good."

"Yeah, man." Killian's hand disappeared, and I heard him sit back in the seat. "When he does come through for us, you're going to have to let that go."

"Nope." Griffin shook his head as his left leg bounced. "I won't. I get that he grew up with you and Sierra and is part of your pack, but I've known him for a couple of years—ever since I started at Shadow University—and I've never been impressed."

"Because he was petrified of you." Killian sighed. "But I know he'll come through. That's all that matters."

"I think he will, too." I pried my fingers under Griffin's, trying to get him to release his death grip on my leg. If he didn't let go, my leg was going to fall asleep. "At least we'll know what we're working with this time."

"I'd feel better if Sierra was here too." Griffin frowned. "If we're walking into a trap, the more people we have, the less risky it will be."

"If she called out or left work early again, that could

make whoever is behind this more suspicious." We couldn't be reactive. We had to keep level heads or the plan wouldn't work.

Killian said, "Don't forget that Dick is already pissed about her missing work the other day. He's been riding her ass ever since."

"Dick riding ass, eh?" I tried lightening the mood in the vehicle. "Why am I not surprised?"

"Dear God," Killian groaned. "Between you and Sierra... Hell, Rosemary even made a similar joke the other day, which freaked me out."

Not even the corner of Griffin's mouth tipped upward, revealing how stressed he really was.

I feel like, ever since you met me, you've been a bottle of nerves. Sometimes I worried that my presence in his life was more problematic than good.

Griffin looked at me for a moment before looking back at the road. *First off, it's only because I care about you so much, but second, I've always been kind of uptight.* He kissed my cheek. *I promise I have never felt happier and more content in my entire life.*

You sure? The scent of a lie was missing, but that couldn't stop me from asking. Each day felt like we were waking up to some sort of hidden threat. *I just don't see how.*

I'm positive, he reassured me as he turned onto the road to the lake. The trees were thick on both sides, taking us to a spot in the lot that the shade from the trees covered. Rosemary and Carter were meeting us in a part of the woods a few miles in the direction that the bear had taken me.

A few visitors would, no doubt, be at the lake, so we were going to meet off the path where no one would see us together.

Griffin pulled into a parking space, and I gazed around. Several people were swimming in the lake. When I opened the door, the grassy and maple scents informed me that the two who seemed to be a couple were bears, and the other four were vampires.

My body tensed. I'd been attacked by two bear shifters already and was feeling particularly wary of them.

The three of us got out of the car, and I grabbed a bag I'd packed for keeping up our charade. Shifters loved to run, so us heading into the woods with extra clothing would help create the façade that we were just there to shift and enjoy the outdoors. This place was only about thirty or so minutes away from Shadow Ridge, so we had to pretend to be there for a day of fun.

Scanning the surroundings, I looked for any crows or falcons; those were the only two birds that could shift into both human and animal forms.

The only thing that stood out was the group of vampires distorting their beautiful faces to scowl in our direction.

I spoke softly, even though we were at least a half-mile away and they wouldn't be able to hear. "Uh...what the hell is their problem?"

"They have to be from Shadow Terrace," Killian spat.

"The town on the other side of the river?" Someone had mentioned it in passing, but not much more. All I knew was that the town was protected by a vampire clan that provided humans to the vampires in Shadow City when needed.

"Yeah. Between us throwing a fit about them funneling humans into Shadow Terrace, and the university being built on our side of the river, things are a little tense between the races." Griffin lifted his chin and ignored the vampires. "Things between us and the vampires are tense inside the city, too. We have conflicting agendas—except for everyone being on board to build the college. However, with so many humans applying and wanting to visit the campus, we didn't want the school located on the vampire side—we knew it would increase the number of human visitors by a lot, and that would be very tempting for them. So, between the wolves and vampires vying for the spot as best protector, and since they both guard a side of the city, the university being located on the wolf side added even more animosity between us."

We stepped into the woods, leaving the scorned vampires behind us. A memory from my first week at the coffee shop passed through my mind. "Doesn't the vampire prince, Alex, attend the university? If there is so much animosity, why is he there?"

"He does, and it's partly to keep an eye on things," Killian said, catching up and walking on my other side. The trees were still spread out enough for us to walk next to one another. "Which was a whole thing within itself. During the first few months the university opened, he fed off one of the humans who was touring the school. Ever since then, a shifter has been assigned to escort every vampire around campus so that doesn't happen again."

"What? Really?" The day I'd met him, he'd seemed nice...but that was part of a vampire's allure. They were manipulative and practiced at hiding their true intentions because darkness was already a part of them. A bloodthirsty monster that tried to make each of them lose their humanity. "He can still walk in the sunlight, or at least tolerate it."

"He's only drunk from the tap a few times." Griffin laughed harshly. "And has never killed anyone. So he's actually pretty clean. Apparently, one of the students had cut the girl or something, trying to make him lose control."

"Wait, they *tried* to make him lose his humanity?" No

wonder Dad said vampires were too corrupt to be around. Granted, I was learning that the shifters and vampires needed the silver wolves' help to suss the vilest people out. Just like how Griffin didn't sense Dick's true intent—if he had, he wouldn't be letting Dick make decisions on his behalf. Maybe the silver wolves leaving the city had been the wrong move after all.

I needed to talk to him about that, but there was always something more pressing going on.

"Yes, Shadow City has come far, but there are still some circles trying to get ahead." Griffin shook his head. "It's hard at times to figure out who is friend or foe."

"This could be a soap opera," I tried teasing, but the joke fell flat. Sometimes the truth wasn't all that funny.

Silence descended between us as the trees thickened. Griffin took the lead, heading to the spot Rosemary had directed us. He reached back and held my hand like he needed to make sure I remained there.

Killian walked behind me, and when I looked back, I saw him glancing around—no doubt looking for any signs that we were being followed or at risk of imminent attack.

I kept my eyes skyward. No way was another damn bird going to spy on us.

Luckily, I didn't see or hear anything suspicious. My heart couldn't help but balloon with hope. Could we actually get ahead of whoever was hunting me after all?

We're almost there, Griffin linked, his pace increasing.

He was as eager to arrive as I was. In fact, I was beyond ready for it all to be over. I'd love to see what a relationship with Griffin would be like without this constant threat hovering over us. I understood his position within the council would always make things tense, and he'd always have enemies, but hopefully not people who'd put our lives at risk every single day.

"Are they there yet?" Griffin asked.

"Yeah," Killian responded. "Carter linked me when we pulled into the lot. They're waiting on us." He chuckled. "He's scared that Rosemary will kill him."

Almost as if on cue, I heard Rosemary's voice. "I swear to God, if you scream like that on the way back, I won't drop you gently."

"You need me," Carter said, cockily. "At least until this is over. I ain't scared."

"You can still do what needs to be done with a broken leg." Rosemary's voice grew deep and threatening. "So don't get cocky."

"You wouldn't." He squeaked. "Dove wouldn't like that."

"Dove isn't my boss." Rosemary retorted. "I don't need her blessing or permission."

Oh, dear God. She was going to make the poor guy piss his pants before we even had a conversation.

The three of us hurried toward them, and I purposely stepped on a branch, hoping that would prevent them from going at it.

"Well, they're on their way," Carter gloated. "So—"

A loud *smack* echoed through the trees.

"Ow!" Carter whined. "You slapped me!"

"Why do you always feel the need to state the obvious?" Rosemary grumbled.

Okay, there went that strategy. Obviously, Rosemary didn't care if we were close. Which wasn't surprising.

The two of them came into view, and Carter was holding a hand over his left cheek.

"I swear the two of you bring out the worst in each other." I shook my head. "And to think you took Rosemary's shit at the coffee shop when I started working there."

"Because I'm a professional." Carter placed his free hand on his chest. "And all bets were off the first time she flew my ass up in the sky. All I could see were clouds, not even the earth below."

"Let's focus," Griffin barked. He stood in front of Carter and crossed his arms, glaring at the guy. "Now spill."

"Fine." Carter lowered his hand. A bright red handprint marked his face.

She'd slapped the shit out of him. I kind of felt bad. Kind of.

"They want it to go down tomorrow." Carter inhaled and winced. "Dude, this still hurts."

Killian rubbed his forehead. "Carter, man, if you know what's best for you, focus."

"They want me to send her out back to take out the garbage around seven in the morning so they can kidnap her before the campus gets busy." Carter took a deep breath. "If they don't get her, my brother loses a hand."

"Well, at least he has another one," Griffin rasped.

"Stop it." I smacked his arm. "He will not, because they're going to capture me."

Griffin's nostrils flared. "Like hell they are."

"If they don't, we won't find out who they are." I wasn't sure what else to do so he would get on board with this. "And they're going to keep attacking. This is the one time we have a heads up on their plan. They take me, and you all will be prepared to follow."

"I can be nearby in a tree." Rosemary nodded and rubbed her fingers together. "I can stay high enough that they won't see me, and I won't lose her." She looked at Griffin. "There will be absolutely no risk of me losing her."

"And you two can be in the parking lot in the car. Hell, we can even rent a car so they won't know it's yours." We had a whole day to plan. We could get a rental car tonight and already have it parked on campus. "You follow us, and worse case, if you can't keep up, Rosemary can text you the location when they stop."

"You expect me to be okay with you being used as bait?" Griffin asked as his forehead wrinkled and his mouth dropped open. He looked completely flabbergasted. "There's no *way* this is going to happen. Tell her, Killian."

Killian lifted a hand. "I'm not thrilled about it, but Dove has a point. This may be the only chance we have the upper hand. We're clueless, and this could lead us straight to the organizer."

I placed a hand on Griffin's chest and turned toward him. "I'm not asking for permission. I *will* be doing this because it's the best plan we have and may be the only time we'll have this kind of advantage. They've been one step ahead of us the whole way. They'll be arrogant and not expect it."

"So, that's the plan." Rosemary nodded. "I promise, Griffin, I won't lose her—and I'll be watching over her so nothing bad happens."

A *kak* sounded, still far away, but my blood ran cold. That was the sound of a falcon.

CHAPTER SEVENTEEN

The scent hadn't hit, and the noise was at least several miles away. Luckily, the falcon couldn't hear us—as birds didn't have exceptional hearing like wolves and angels —but their vision was better.

"We need to get out of here before that falcon finds us." Granted, the bird might not be working for our enemy—but we couldn't risk it. "Rosemary, when you get back to Griffin's, we can make more concrete plans. It's probably better if Carter doesn't know the details in case anyone comes poking around ahead of time."

"True," Rosemary agreed and picked up Carter, throwing him over her shoulder as her black wings sprouted from her back.

"What the—" he gasped, and she placed a hand over his mouth as his eyes grew wide. She took flight, using the trees as cover, flying in the opposite direction from the bird. She flapped her wings hard and disappeared from our sights within seconds.

Killian chuckled. "That was one way of handling it."

"At least she knew to stay hidden, but we better change the subject." I walked back toward the Navigator.

"Shouldn't we stay out here for a little while?" Killian asked as he glanced at the sky. "Not that I want to."

Ideally, we would go deeper into the woods for a hike to keep up our pretenses. "The bird could be leading others over to attack us. Maybe they caught on that Carter was alerting us to their plans and this was the true strategy." Too much was at risk to stay, including the memories that haunted Killian.

"You're right." Killian nodded.

Let me take the lead. You're the one they're after, so please let me lead with Killian following you. Griffin moved in front, not bothering to wait for my answer.

I wanted to argue, because he'd only pretended to run that by me, but we didn't have time to spare. All it would potentially do was put us in more danger, and I cared too much about these two to let pride get in my way. I swallowed the hurt feelings, even though the lump in my throat refused to go down. Being an alpha wolf myself, I didn't like people taking decisions away from me.

I stayed between the two men, focusing on getting back to the car. We moved at a much quicker pace than we had when entering the woods, so if the bird caught up to us, we'd be safely around others.

The next *kak* sounded much closer because he did have the advantage of traveling through the sky, but he wasn't gaining as much on us as he might expect. The three of us were comfortable in nature, and even in unfamiliar territory, we could cover a lot of ground quickly.

Water splashing could be heard, which meant that we were nearing the lake with the bears and the vampires.

Right now, they'd be a welcome sight...even with the vampires' hateful expressions.

When the trees began to thin, my heart returned to a normal rhythm. We would definitely make it back before anyone could attack.

Sprinting even faster, we reached the tree line in minutes. Griffin slowed down before the other supernaturals could see us. They'd probably heard our approach, but that shouldn't seem odd due to the kind of supernaturals we were. The only thing that might seem strange was the short amount of time we'd been gone; wolves tended to enjoy running for a while, not minutes.

As expected, the vampires looked at us with varying puzzled expressions. One was visibly upset, stroking his short beard while watching us the entire way to the vehicle.

The three of us pretended to not notice their stares, our focus on getting to the Navigator. When my hand clutched the door handle, the falcon flew overhead.

Unable to stop myself, I looked up and saw a mostly white-feathered falcon. He didn't seem to be paying any attention to us as he swooped down toward the bear shifter couple, who were locked in a lingering kiss.

He landed right in the girl's thick black hair, causing her to jerk back and swat at him. She yelled, "Ollie! What the hell?"

As I climbed into the vehicle, my body sagged in the seat. I was so paranoid, every bird shifter was potentially evil. That was how prejudice started—but right now we had to be careful. When this was all over, I would befriend some bird shifters and prove to myself that most of them were good.

Dad had told me over and over that the main problem with our supernatural world was that we were still segregated; we lived independently from one another and came together only when necessary. When I first got to Shadow Ridge, I'd found his words hard to believe, especially that first day at the university. The place was full of all kinds of supernaturals, and I knew the council was a mixed bag as well. But the longer I stayed, the more his words began to make sense. Each race was fighting for their best interests and not for the greater good of the community. Shadow City had started as a refuge, but when the angels took over, they'd recruited and let in only the strongest supernaturals in the world. The original intent of a safe haven had been thrown out the door.

"All that, and he came to hang out with bear shifters." Killian shut his door. "I'm not complaining, though. I'd rather we be severely risk-averse and alive instead of the alternative."

"Now that's something we agree on." Griffin put the car in drive. "I feel like we haven't been on the same page lately."

"Why? Because of Carter?" Killian huffed.

I did *not* want to hear this argument again. "That's the only thing you two disagree on. So please, stop. I don't have the energy to listen to you bicker like an old married couple again."

No one responded, and Griffin placed his hand back on my thigh.

You better be glad I love you, Griffin teased, and pretended to glare at me. *Because if I didn't, I might accuse you of taking his side.*

I've made it clear that I agree with him on this one. I kissed his cheek, not wanting to truly upset him. *So, there.*

Yeah, I know. He watched the road once again, and the rest of the ride was silent.

"Where the hell is she?" Griffin paced in front of the couch and loveseat. "You'd think she'd be back by now."

"Chill." Sierra snorted as she plopped next to me on the loveseat, taking Griffin's usual spot. She smelled of grease from her shift at the bar. "I've only been here for ten minutes, and you've already got me so tense that I might snap at any second."

"That's my spot," he growled and pointed at her.

"You weren't sitting here." She stuck out her tongue. "That means it's fair game."

Moments like these were my favorite. These were the small pockets of time where things felt almost normal. They were the ones that gave me enough hope and strength to waddle through the shit. A little bit of clarity among the chaos.

Killian entered the room with the burger Sierra had brought for him. "Did you roll around in the fryer before coming here? We could smell the grease on you before you even walked in."

"Don't hate." She lifted her head high. "Unlike you two, some of us have to serve bar food in order to make ends meet."

"Hey, we work hard, too." Killian gestured his burger in my direction. "It's a full-time job keeping this one alive. I swear I've never worked this hard, even when Dad was alive."

"Does that mean when things calm down, you're officially going to take over?" Sierra tugged at her bottom lip. "The both of you?"

I already knew Griffin's answer, but I'd never directly

asked Killian. We didn't get alone time as we had before, with Griffin, Rosemary, and Sierra always around.

"Sterlyn and I have already discussed this." Griffin winked at me. "When we've taken down the enemy, we're going to continue Dad's original plans and make some of our own."

"Really?" She faced me. "I love this. You two will make a fierce team." She leaned closer to me and whispered, despite her voice still being loud enough for Griffin and Killian to hear, "Honestly, you're the one I'm excited to see lead. You keep his head on straight...and girl power."

"I'm standing right here," Griffin deadpanned.

"Oh, she knows." I bumped my shoulder into hers. "She's trying to get a rise out of you."

"True, but I did mean it." Sierra blew her bangs out of her face and focused on Killian. "Now, what about you?"

"Yeah, I think it's time I stop being afraid." Killian inhaled. "It's important that we protect this part of Shadow City, and with Griffin and Sterlyn in charge, I feel like it's time for me to step up and take my rightful place. How do you think Billy is going to take it?"

Sierra snorted loudly. "He'll be dancing the macarena."

Killian pursed his lips. "You think so?"

"Don't get me wrong, he's been a great leader in your absence, but he doesn't have that alpha edge." Sierra shrugged. "You'll be fine. He is an amazing second-hand. Your dad always said so."

Feet landed outside the back door, and Rosemary entered the house.

"What the hell took you so long?" Griffin bellowed as he pivoted toward her.

He should have known better than to talk to her that way. The angel wouldn't put up with that kind of attitude.

"Excuse me?" Rosemary turned her head in his direction and pointed at her ear. "I did hear 'thank you,' and 'how did everything go', right?"

"No." Sierra leaned forward, shaking her head wildly. "You did not. In fact, you heard—"

"He might not have said it, but I will." We didn't need to alienate the one person who gave us an edge—especially when the other side had crows, bear shifters, and wolves. And those were the ones we knew about. "Thank you. I hope Carter didn't drive you too insane on the flight back to wherever you dropped him off." He lived somewhere in this neighborhood, but I didn't know where.

"Oh, it went fine." A rare smile flitted across her face, making her even more breathtaking. "Covering his mouth was something I should've done from the get-go, and I may have given him a little hint of what could happen if I have to take him somewhere again and he screams."

Killian frowned, but that didn't stop him from taking another huge bite of his burger. With a full mouth, he asked, "Wha dijoo do?"

"I may have dropped him from ten feet up when he whimpered loudly." Rosemary rubbed her ears. "I can't handle him being a freaking lunatic anymore. I think he learned his lesson."

"Did he get hurt?" He shouldn't have, but with Carter, anything was possible.

"No. It may have stung a little when his feet hit the ground." She shrugged. "No biggie."

"Can we focus here?" Griffin massaged his temples. "We need to make sure we have a solid plan for tomorrow. I am personally against this plan, but obviously, I'm outvoted."

"Outvoted doesn't matter." This was my decision. No one else's. "I'm the one putting my life at risk."

"Exactly," Griffin growled.

"What about that bird?" Rosemary asked, and then snatched Killian's burger from his hands. She took a large bite out of it before handing it back to him and sitting on the other side of the couch.

He blinked several times, looking from his burger to the angel. "What the hell just happened?"

"What?" Rosemary asked and lifted both hands. "I'm hungry."

Sierra laughed. "I brought you a burger too. It's in the kitchen."

"Thank God." Rosemary sighed. "Because that's really good."

"It's from Dick's." Sierra wrinkled her nose. "Which I hate to say, but see—if you angels tried some of the shifter restaurants, you might find that you like them."

Even though shifters would eat at each other's restaurants, we still kept to our own races. No other supernaturals frequented shifter establishments.

A pink hue tinted Griffin's face.

He might spontaneously combust if we didn't keep on track. This was hard enough on him even without their squirrel moments. "We're pretty sure the falcon wasn't spying or scouting us out. He playfully attacked a bear shifter couple who were making out."

"Okay, good. But I'll be careful and go to campus early to scan for any suspicious birds or anything else before I hide in a tree." Rosemary licked her lips. "We all need to take precautions."

"We rented a car on the way home." Griffin's jaw twitched. "And parked it in the lot. Killian and Sierra will get there early, as well, and I'll sneak over after walking Sterlyn in like normal."

Rosemary nodded. "Good—that's key. We have to make everything appear completely normal."

Easier said than done. Tomorrow morning, I'd be riddled with anxiety...but I'd have to hide it. "So, I play the part of the unsuspecting target." I only hoped that I didn't wind up in a trunk again. That had been horrible and hot.

"How the hell is Carter going to pull off you taking out the garbage?" Sierra sat back and crossed her legs. "I mean, every business that serves food takes the garbage out each night. How is he going to justify a morning trash run?"

"That isn't my problem." I shrugged, at a loss.

"It's Carter." A vein in Griffin's neck stuck out. "You can't count on him to figure out something like that. He's an idiot."

"In all fairness, he did get me into the supply closet and drug me." I hated to admit it, but the truth was just that.

The truth.

"I'm sure we can find something to throw out." One more thing to determine in the morning.

Can I talk to you? Griffin asked, his mesmerizing eyes locking with mine as his feelings of anxiety and worry slammed into me. *Alone?*

Crap. *Of course.* I stood, wishing I could tell him no. But I couldn't. I knew how concerned he was about this plan, and I needed to hear him out. I just hoped the rest of our night wouldn't be ruined.

CHAPTER EIGHTEEN

I followed Griffin into our bedroom while the other two stayed with Rosemary as she ate her dinner. Luckily, we'd eaten our food prior to Rosemary getting here.

Well, correction... Killian and I ate while Griffin glared at him. I could feel how much this all bothered him, but there wasn't a damn thing I could do about it. When I looked at it from every angle, this strategy was what I kept coming back to.

When I entered the room, Griffin shut the door behind me a little too hard. The doorframe shuddered at the force.

I'd been expecting his outburst, having felt it brewing inside him ever since Carter made the call informing us that the enemy had contacted him. For a second, I'd falsely hoped that we wouldn't argue. Hell, we hadn't officially had our first fight.

I guessed that changed now.

I want you to call this off. Griffin jumped right to the point. *This is a bad decision. You being captured isn't the right answer.* His hazel eyes darkened to all brown, as if the warm green flecks had simply disappeared.

I kept a clear head and didn't react as I wanted to because I had to put myself in his shoes. If he'd suggested using himself as bait, I wouldn't be thrilled, either. In fact, I would be doing everything possible to find a different course of action. But, unlike him, I would see the plan for what it was—our best chance.

This, again, went back to him not having the same battle strategy training I'd had my entire life. Without that training on his side, I would have to help him see things in a different light. *Okay, then what do you suggest?*

His head tipped backward as the tension around his eyes slackened. He nibbled on his bottom lip as his brows furrowed in confusion.

He hadn't expected me to respond like that. He'd been prepared to argue.

Uh... Well, I can get Dick involved and see if he can help us find the culprit. Griffin nodded like he was convincing himself that what he said was the best course of action.

Dammit, I understood his gut reaction, but I needed to figure out a way to help him decide that it wasn't a good idea to include that bastard. *So, you want to put the person who is currently running Shadow City at risk and potentially lose not one council member, but two?* The words tasted sour in my mind, but talking down to him wouldn't work. Dad had used this strategy with me while I was growing up, and I believed it had helped me learn to think things through more objectively. *I'm not sure he has our best interests at heart. I have a feeling about him.*

Fine. Okay. I trust you. He blew out a breath as he ran his fingers into his now disheveled honey-brown hair. *Then we wait until they contact Carter again when he doesn't deliver you. Maybe you can say that was an odd morning request and you have other things to do.*

They won't give Carter a second chance, and he would be more likely to inform them that we knew the plans and that he was compromised in order to save his brother. Not to mention his brother probably will lose a hand or worse. I sat on the bed and placed my hands in my lap, staring straight ahead. *Then they could attack us again, knowing that we lost our temporary advantage over them.*

Then we fight. Griffin nodded as he sat next to me. *And you can stay somewhere safe like Shadow City in the meantime.*

And leave others here to fight when these people are coming for me? That was the one option that I would never accept, even if Griffin tried to demand it. *What kind of leader would that make me? If we want to lead Shadow City, side by side, that strategy is the worst option. No one would respect me or be able to view me as their alpha or, hell, even the alpha's mate.*

His hands clutched mine to the point of near pain. He practically yelled through our bond, *Who fucking cares? At least you'd be alive and safe!*

My wolf growled, infuriated that he'd spoken to us that way. We weren't his pack member, but his equal. If I wanted to, I could force him to submit to me. But the silver wolves weren't meant to lead regular wolves. They were meant to lead the other protectors and make the calls that were the most difficult to make.

War strategies.

Like these. But I would never talk down to him and insult him that way. Even if he had just done that to me. His reaction stemmed from emotions and caring; a good place, even if it was uncalled for.

Look. I tried to stay level-headed, but my irritation bled through. *I can only imagine what you're feeling.* I turned my body and fully faced him, cupping his cheek with one hand. Our eyes caught and held. *But your people not respecting me isn't an option. My dad raised me to be the kind of warrior that people would respect, and what you're asking me to do is something that would make him turn over in his grave.* If he had one. That was yet another thing I had to figure out—what those assholes had done to my pack's bodies. If I could find them, I wanted to give each and every one of them a proper burial, as any shifter and fighter deserved.

The anger faded from his eyes, and his whole body sagged in defeat. *I'm sorry. I didn't mean to do that, but the thought of you walking into something and getting hurt when I could've done something to prevent it...it almost paralyzes me.*

His honesty was what I needed to get to the root of the problem. *But you have to know this is the strategy that makes the most sense—and asking me not to do it isn't right. I get that we're mates, but I'm still an individual who believes this is the best decision. I'm not trying to be a martyr. I don't have a death wish. In fact, because of you, I'm determined to make it out of this alive. But I need you to trust me and my instincts.*

You weren't supposed to argue with me. He leaned his forehead against mine and continued, *Or use logic.*

I'll always listen to your concerns. He was my mate, and even if I didn't agree with him, he deserved the respect of being heard. *I love you.*

He ran his fingers through my hair and kissed me. The feelings of love between the two of us intermingled as we opened to each other to show how much we cared.

You are something I never prepared for. He pulled back, locking on to my gaze. *Had I known what was tugging at me that morning in the coffee shop, I would've tried not to be such an ass to you. You didn't deserve to be talked to that way.*

I smiled, remembering his cringe-worthy pickup lines. *Our first conversation was not a good way to introduce yourself, but I wouldn't have it any other way. After all, I got to tell you right away that I wouldn't take that shit from you.*

He chuckled. *I didn't know how to react. I never had a girl shoot me down like that before, and then Killian walked in, marking his territory.* He shuddered. *I almost tore him a new asshole right then and there.*

At least, you didn't pee on me, I teased. To think about how our relationship had changed since then was crazy. He was now my other half in all of the ways that mattered. The thought of being without him terrified me.

He kissed me again. *Oh, believe me, I thought about it. In fact...* He grabbed my waist and hoisted me onto my back on the bed before crawling on top of me. He took both of my wrists, and placed them beside my head, holding me in place. *Maybe I should do it now.*

No, he wouldn't. *You've bitten me. I think we're good.*

Better safe than sorry, he said as he raked his teeth against my neck.

My body heated between being restrained and the slight pain. *I'm okay with how you're making sure.*

This time we get to go slow. He sucked hard, making his intentions of leaving a hickey obvious.

For some reason, the fact that he wanted to mark me thrilled me. The bruise would be gone by morning, but the effort he put forth for even a temporary branding excited me in ways I'd never imagined.

His hand slipped under my shirt, then my bra, and

pinched my nipple. I inhaled sharply as the two sensations overwhelmed my senses.

Is this okay? he asked, caressing my breast more firmly.

I nodded, not able to speak even in my mind.

He kissed his way down my neck slowly and lifted my shirt. His mouth replaced his fingers as his teeth scraped against me.

A low moan escaped, but I wasn't embarrassed. I tried pushing against him, but his hand kept me secured in place.

Instead of loosening his grip, he bit down, which had me bucking beneath him.

Take me, I growled, primed and ready for him.

No, he said sternly. *Not yet. I'll be in agony tomorrow, so it's your turn tonight.*

What the hell? I couldn't believe that he'd say something like that—but then his tongue began to work, making my mind foggy. Need flowed through me, short-circuiting my brain.

He released the hold on one of my wrists and rolled to the side as his hand slid down to my jeans and unbuttoned them. Within seconds, his fingers were between my legs, rubbing and setting my body on fire.

The glorious torture of his mouth and hand was unlike anything I'd ever experienced. My body quivered with powerful desire. *Griffin,* I whispered, not above begging. *Please.*

He removed his hand and stood, dragging my pants and panties away from my body as he moved. After they lay crumpled on the floor, he discarded his own.

He pulled his shirt from his body, and I enjoyed watching his six-pack contract. My mate was the sexiest man I'd ever seen, and the fact that he was all mine added to the lust coursing through me.

I lifted high enough so I could yank my shirt off. I wanted to feel his skin on mine; it was the best sensation in the world. He snaked a hand around me, unfastening my bra and tossing it aside.

Ready for him, I moved to spin around, but he caught my waist, holding me in place.

I get to be in control this time. He slid between my legs and thrust deep inside me.

Throwing my head back, I wrapped my legs around his waist, and he moved in and out slowly—over and over again. He captured my breast in his mouth as he continued in a slow but strong pace, making tension build steadily inside me. I'd thought the emotions coming fast and furious couldn't be matched, but this was intense in a different kind of way. No matter how I tried to quicken the pace, he held firm.

The sensation strengthened inside me, overwhelming me. The intensity of the friction both hurt and felt amazing. I dug my fingers into his back, and a sharp metallic smell hit me as warm drops of blood puddled under my nails.

"Oh, God," I groaned, as he finally began to increase the rhythm. His body shook as an orgasm rocked through both of us. His thrusting became quicker, pounding even deeper inside me. My body contracted as the strongest release shook me. My head went light, and my vision blurred.

He slowed as we both came down from our shared high. His lips devoured me as he chuckled in my mind, *I told you you'd call me that.*

It took a second for his meaning to sink in. That first time he saw me, he'd told me I'd be calling him God later that night. I giggled and smacked his arm, rolling him off me. I arched an eyebrow as I growled, "You better be glad I love you."

"Oh, I am," he said seriously, as he pulled me into his arms. "I'm happier about that than you'll ever know."

THE NEXT MORNING, Griffin walked me into the coffee shop. His grip on my hand was extra tight, mirroring the fear and anxiety that riddled him.

We'd enjoyed our night together, but his chaotic emotions had woken me up this morning. If I were a betting person, I'd put money on him not having slept at all.

Hey, Rosemary called and told us she doesn't see or sense anything out of the ordinary, and she's in the tree. I tried reassuring him because I hated that my decision was causing him to feel this way. *Killian and Sierra are in the rental car, and you'll be with them soon.*

Just promise me that if anything we haven't prepared for happens, you'll let me know. He rolled his shoulders, at least trying to act normal. *And that you'll be okay with me stepping in if there's any indication that we won't be able to follow you, or if the danger escalates.*

As long as you make sure it's not you being overly paranoid. If he could promise me that, I'd be okay.

Some of the tension did leave his body, and he faced me. *Really?*

I trust you. I kissed him and forced myself to walk behind the counter and put on an apron. *So, if you truly believe something isn't going as expected, then do what you feel like you need to.*

"Oh, look." Carter's voice cracked, and there was sweat on his upper lip. "Your boyfriend is here...again."

His attempt to sound normal was coming across more as scared. Someone was probably watching us, given the kidnapping was supposed to take place in the next little bit. I hoped they'd expected Carter to be nervous.

"Mate." Griffin tried to sound annoyed, but his delivery fell a little flatter than normal.

Hopefully, if anyone was close enough to hear, they wouldn't notice.

"You two be nice." I tied the apron and shook my head, trying to act better than them. "One day, you're going to wind up friends."

"Fat chance." Griffin wrinkled his nose and scowled at Carter.

You need to leave. For the plan to work, he had to go get breakfast like he normally did. *I know it's hard, but after today, this should all be over.* At least, that was the goal.

I love you. He kissed me again, lingering a few seconds too long. *This is the hardest thing I have ever had to do in my entire life, and it proves I'm willing to do anything for you.*

Brushing my fingertips across his cheek, I smiled. *You proved it the time you jumped in front of that gun to protect me.* I was talking about the ambush we'd survived together in the woods outside his and Killian's houses just one day before I was abducted.

And that wasn't a hard decision at all. He kissed my fingertips and looked at me a second longer. *You better come home to me.* He pivoted and walked out the door.

I'd prepared to get hurt and be put in threatening situations, but I hadn't been prepared for how damn hard it would be to watch Griffin walk away. Even though I knew this was the best strategy, there was a chance that I might not see him again.

"Hey, Dove." Carter cleared his throat. "I forgot to take out one of the trash bags yesterday afternoon. Would you run it out back before the others get here? I'd hate for them to think it's okay to slack off."

My heart sank. His request had come sooner than we'd planned. *I'm heading out to the dumpster now.*

What? Griffin sounded tense. *I'm not in the car yet. Take as long as you can so I can get there. I need five minutes.*

Carter mouthed 'I'm sorry. They texted me a few minutes ago.'

Dammit. He was being an idiot. *They changed the time on him.*

We need to abort. Griffin sounded tense. *They could be suspicious.*

No, they're just being careful. It was something I would do if I were them. *It's smart.* I took the bag from Carter. "Okay, but I won't cover for your ass again."

I walked through the kitchen, taking my time. *Are you there yet?*

Yes, I just got into the car. I wasn't followed—I went out a side door I never use, he rasped. *Killian started the car. We're ready.*

All right. It was time.

I pushed open the back door and stepped out...and someone grabbed me from behind, spinning me in the direction of the garbage can so I couldn't see them. Before I could even scream, a cloth bag went over my head, obstructing my vision.

There was no going back now.

CHAPTER NINETEEN

My wolf took over, and I yanked against the man holding my arms. It would be suspicious if I didn't try to fight him off...but that wasn't why I was doing it. I didn't like being confined with my vision taken away.

The full moon was approaching, which meant I was growing stronger each day. I almost broke free, but managed to rein myself in.

Barely.

Griffin's face popped into my head, which made me remember what was at stake. If I ruined this abduction attempt, there was no telling what other attacks would happen—and who might die as a result. So many of Killian's and Griffin's men had already died because of me.

Fingers dug into my arm as the man held me tight. The smell of grass hit my nose, telling me that this was a bear shifter.

"Open the car door before she breaks free," the guy growled.

The voice was all too familiar to me, although I'd heard it only once before.

From the horrible frosted-tips bear who'd attacked me at Dick's bar.

I knew now that the attack hadn't been some sort of attempt to instigate a civil war as Dick and Griffin had assumed about Shadow City and its affiliated civilians. According to them, people were rioting due to the opening of the gates, and shifters were attacking their own kind.

The faint musky smell of a wolf shifter coated the air, and a few seconds later, a door opened.

"Let me go," I growled. Playing the part of an angry wolf shifter wasn't hard; rage coursed through me in sync with my heartbeat. I tamped down my extreme desire to escape, trying to keep a level head. I took a deep breath like I'd been taught, but it didn't help. It was humid and dark, and I was breathing more carbon monoxide than oxygen, adding to my panic rather than relieving it.

Frosted Tips chuckled darkly. "Not going to happen."

The enjoyment in his tone rattled me to the core as the cold realization that he was as twisted as Dick filled me.

When someone shoved me toward the car, I almost stumbled, but somehow managed to stay upright. I had no clue what kind of vehicle we were getting into or who was in it. Even though I hadn't wanted to get in the trunk, I wasn't quite sure getting in the car with God knew who would be better. At least in the trunk, I'd be alone.

The musky smell tickled my nose again as the wolf shifter gasped, "Wait. Her hands. We need to bind them unless you plan on her sitting in your lap the entire way there."

God, please, no. I yanked against his hold again as my skin crawled. I didn't want to sit in anyone's lap.

"Calm down," Frosted Tips growled. "You're hot, but I know you pack a mean punch." His weight shifted, and he addressed the wolf again, "There are some handcuffs in the front—grab them, and let's restrain her."

"On it." His footsteps rushed only a couple of feet before another door opened.

This had to be a smaller car, which kind of surprised me. I'd figured they'd have several men with them, but maybe, like the other bear shifter, they expected this to be an easy job and didn't have more backup. That was a good thing. Maybe their numbers would be small—wherever they were taking me—since they thought I was subdued.

The quick shuffling of feet headed back toward us, and within seconds, my hands were yanked behind my back, and cool metal was fastened around my wrists. When Frosted Tips released my arm, a little bit of sanity came back to me. Some of the desperate need to escape was gone.

A large hand shoved me, making me fall forward in shock. Luckily, I hit the seat of the car instead of landing on the ground. With my hands behind my back, I could've been severely injured.

"Get all the way in, now," Frosted Tips demanded. "We've got to go. We've been here too long. That pathetic alpha wolf is probably already almost here. She must have linked him right away."

I stayed put, pretending to try to drag the whole situation out like he was right.

Large hands grabbed my waist and placed me on my ass. He grabbed my legs and tossed them inside. I tried to stick them back out, but he slammed the door, causing it to hit my ankle. Pain radiated for a second, but it'd only clipped the side. It should be healed in minutes.

"I know what you're trying to do," he said disgustedly from outside my window, knowing I could hear me. "And it's not happening."

When the front door opened, I startled. I'd expected the bear to be driving, but instead, I heard him climb into the passenger seat.

Tires squealed as the car jolted forward.

"Dammit, you're going to alert everyone around to us," Frosted Tips snapped, clearly not impressed. "Maybe you should pull over and let me drive."

"And waste more time?" Clearly, the wolf had had enough of being talked down to. "We're good. Besides, the campus is pretty much dead. Most students opt for later classes these days."

"Yeah, but her mate is around." Frosted Tips snorted. "So trying to stay below the radar is our best damn strategy."

"We're pulling out of the university now. Slow your damn roll," the wolf bit back.

Please tell me you're okay. Griffin's comforting voice filled my head.

That was subjective, but I was in the back seat alone. I didn't sense anyone else around me...and at the moment, I'd call that a win. *I'm fine. Please tell me that you guys are in place.*

Yeah, we're hanging back, but you're in our vision. The tension was so thick from him that he could've been sitting right beside me. *Do you know who they are?*

Well, they were waiting for me as soon as the door opened, and they put a bag over my head. At least, when I'd been thrown in the trunk, my head hadn't been covered. *But I recognized one of the voices. It's the bear shifter who attacked me in the bar.*

So he's working with the ones hunting you. That's how the bastard got away. Griffin spoke so low through our link that it was hard to hear. *I'll kill him...slowly.*

Now wasn't the time to focus on torture. No matter how appealing it sounded. *Just make sure you don't ride too close. They mentioned you, saying they needed to get me out of there before you caught on to me being gone. So they're paranoid.*

They should be. When we get there, I'll put a bullet in their heads first thing.

Wait, when did you pack guns?

Killian brought them this morning. Griffin sounded offended. *Do you think you're the only one who can make smart decisions? We were surprised when you didn't bring it up.*

Because I didn't want to risk it if we were being watched. It didn't matter now. They'd done it, and these two idiots appeared none the wiser. *But I'm glad you did. We have no clue what we're walking into.*

Remember, I wasn't thrilled with this plan, to begin with. But I got outvoted, and you had your mind made up.

He was right. I did. And I didn't regret it.

Let me see if I can weasel out any information that might help us. Any sort of heads-up we could get as to what we were walking into would be helpful.

Just be careful. Griffin pleaded.

Always. I love you.

He sighed. *I love you too—that's why I'm struggling so damn hard.*

I know. That wasn't new information. *And I'm sorry. I'm going to work these two and hope they aren't smart.* I turned my attention away from Griffin and closed my eyes. There was no reason to keep them open, it didn't make a bit of difference. "So...where are we headed?"

"That's none of your concern," Frosted Tips snapped. "Do you really think we'd tell you something like that? I bet you're already linked to your mate, begging him to come find you and save your life."

"I don't know what you're talking about?" The sulfuric stench of my lie filled the car.

"Oh, God." The wolf coughed and rolled down the window. "You'd think she'd know there was no point in doing that."

"She's a woman." Frosted Tips chuckled. "She doesn't know any better. They're born stupid."

He was trying to rile me up, but I refused to play along. Instead, I focused on the breeze whipping around me. I pretended that I could actually breathe the fresh air through the bag on my head, trying to use my deep breathing technique to help calm my racing heart.

My wolf was angry and scared, not liking that we were acting weak. She was used to dominating, and being complaisant went against everything ingrained in us. Dad had wanted us to prove these sexist assholes wrong, not bend to their will. I tried to reassure her that it was just another strategy of war, but she wasn't appeased.

Honestly, neither was I.

"So... how did you escape from that car?" I forced my voice to shake a little like I was petrified and trying to be strong. I needed them to underestimate me. That would make things easier when the time came to act.

"Once again, not answering," Frosted Tips said with annoyance. "Why are you asking questions?"

He was smarter than I hoped. That was unfortunate.

"I can't wait to see her reaction," the wolf babbled. "It's going to be epic."

"Why?" That didn't sound good. My breathing quickened, and I hoped they'd think it was due to the bag and not fear.

A loud *smack* sounded, shocking me. The car swerved like the driver had lost control for a second.

"Why the hell did you hit me?" the wolf growled. "You touch me again, and I'll kick your ass. I don't care if you're twice my size."

"Don't be a dumbass, then." Frosted Tips didn't sound scared or threatened. "You're running your mouth, which is dangerous. All it takes is one little slip, and her mate could figure it out. We have to get her far enough away that he can't use the mate bond to find her."

Whoever was making the calls had thought it through. They knew Griffin and I were mated and that they'd need to put enough distance between us to slow him down. If Carter hadn't alerted us, I would have been screwed. I also had a feeling they had backup in case I did break free again.

There was no point in continuing the conversation. I'd have to let events take their course if I wanted to learn anything.

TIME MUST HAVE STOPPED. There was no other explanation. My numb ass and sweaty face were almost too much to bear. Sweat puddled between my breasts as the heat took me to the point of almost suffocating.

I was sure there was plenty of oxygen, but I'd been under the bag for so long I was dizzy. I laid my head on the back of the seat, trying to let a breeze in from the bottom. No such luck.

All I got for the effort was a crick in my neck.

The car slowed and turned onto another road. The sounds of gravel crunching under the wheels told me we were likely close to our destination. *Hey, I think we're getting close to wherever we're heading.*

Yeah, we see that. Griffin sounded nearly unhinged. *I swear, if anything happens to you before we can get there—*

His concern warmed my heart, and I wished I could take his discomfort away. Unfortunately, I was hanging on by a thread too. The entire ride had been torture, and neither one of them had spoken again, so I'd had absolutely nothing to distract me. I hadn't wanted to talk to Griffin because all it would do would be to rile him up more, which would result in bad decisions.

We couldn't risk that, so I cut him off. *Rosemary will be there if I need help before you arrive.* He tended to forget we had more people helping us and it wasn't all up to him to save me.

You're right, but, please, keep me informed on what's going on. His thoughts broke. *We've pulled over, and we're getting out now. We'll be there soon.*

The ride became bumpier, causing my neck to jar. I sat up straight, bending my head side to side while wiggling my fingers. I needed to get my body ready to fight. I was pretty sure if I channeled my wolf hard enough, I could break through the handcuffs.

As the car slowed, my heart picked up its pace.

"We're here," the wolf shifter said as he shifted the car into park. "You're going to take her, right?"

"Yeah," Frosted Tips growled as he opened his door.

Mine soon opened as well, and he curled his fingers around my arm and yanked me out of the car. I fell on the gravel, but luckily, my jeans protected my legs.

"Oh, sorry about that," he deadpanned, the insincerity of his words clear.

"It's about damn time that the two of you got here," a

deep voice rasped as feet pounded into the gravel. "I thought you fucked up retrieving her again."

The bear's hold tightened, yet again. "I don't underestimate my enemy more than once."

"You shouldn't do it the very first time, either." The new guy sounded disgusted, and his musky pine smell tickled a memory in the back of my head. Did I know him?

"Are you planning on standing here and insulting me, or are you going to tell me where to put her?" Frosted Tips snarled.

I needed the damn bag off my head. I tried climbing to my feet and pushed my pride aside as I fell.

"Wow." The deeper voice sounded unimpressed. "She outsmarted you once? Why aren't there holes in the bag for her to breathe? And how long have you left the bag over her head?"

"He left it on her the entire way," the wolf gloated. "And he said she didn't need air."

Footsteps moved closer, and I could hear the new guy squat in front of me. His hand grabbed the bottom of the bag, and he removed the material from my face.

I sucked in a breath, trying to clear my head, but when I looked into this new person's face, my heart and lungs stopped working.

Squatting before me was a younger version of Dad. His silver hair was a little darker than mine, and his silver eyes were the exact shade of my father's. That was why he smelled so familiar—his scent was a combination of Mom's and Dad's. Just like mine.

There was only one explanation as to who he was...but it was impossible. "I thought you were dead."

CHAPTER TWENTY

"Oh, did you now?" The man chuckled. "You expect me to believe that?" His eyes hardened, turning a granite color.

He had to be kidding, but my mind sputtered, not quite able to catch up with this development. *I think I'm looking at my dead brother. Cyrus.* I had to say the words, and my gut told me that saying them out loud was the wrong move. "You'd know if I were lying."

When she'd gone to clean us both up, the witch who'd attended our birth had told my father that my brother had died...and yet, this man was standing here in front of me, and the resemblance couldn't be denied. Something tingled inside my chest, and I had no clue what the hell it could be.

Your brother? Griffin sounded as bewildered as I felt. *The one who died at birth?*

The very one. I mean, I'm not absolutely sure, but he looks like Dad and smells like him and Mom. Like me.

Frosted Tips scratched his head and glanced back and forth between the man and me. "You two know each other?"

"No, we don't," Maybe-Cyrus spat.

"I can't keep up." The wolf kicked at the ground, making a dust cloud. His cornflower-blue eyes filled with confusion as a slight breeze ruffled his pecan-colored hair. He wasn't nearly as large as my brother or Griffin but more slender and athletic, reminding me of Carter. "She said you were dead, so how do you two not know each other, Julius?" Scrawny looked small compared to the other two guys.

Frosted Tips crossed his thick, hairy arms over his massive chest, straining the top two buttons of his shirt where even more chest hair spilled out. Just like I remembered, his hair was an awful vanilla color on the tips, with dark-brown everywhere else. His long, dark-brown beard reached the top of his chest hair, and he puffed out his chest —which made him look nearly the size of a truck. He wasn't much larger than Cyrus, though.

"It's none of your damn business," Cyrus retorted, and turned his hate-filled gaze back on me. "I'm taking her inside. You two idiots keep an eye out for anything that seems abnormal. We can't be too careful since she went and got fucking mated. Like that was actually going to save her." He chuckled nastily.

He was definitely a silver wolf...but maybe he wasn't my brother. Scrawny had called him Julius—which wasn't my brother's name—and he wasn't old enough to be my uncle. Maybe he was a cousin? Various ideas ran through my head. Negativity rolled off him, but it wasn't as overwhelming as the bear's or Dick's, so maybe there was hope. "You think I was trying to save myself and that's why I got mated?" I focused on the safest topic.

"That's what I would've done." He shrugged his shoulders. "But the boss wants you whether you're tainted or not. I mean...he doesn't want you for love."

Frosted Tips growled. "Get one of your flunkies to stand guard. My ass—"

Julius almost blurred as he rushed the bear and punched the guy's jaw. The force of the impact caused the bear shifter to fall back on his ass and clutch his face.

Even though it was daylight, the silver moon would soon be upon us. The power of that moon was already sizzling through my blood, so it had to be doing the same thing inside Julius.

"One more word and I'll withhold your pay and get the joy of teaching you a lesson." Julius's nostrils flared as he stood over the bear. "Got it?"

"Yes." Frosted Tips nodded so fast I was surprised his neck didn't crack. "We'll stand guard." He averted his gaze to the ground.

"If he gives you any lip..." He turned to Scrawny. "You let me or one of the guards in the house know. I will not have any of my men challenge me."

My stomach dropped. I didn't know why I hadn't realized it immediately—probably because of his familiarity—but this silver wolf was in charge. Which shouldn't be possible. We were born inherently good and were protectors of good for all supernaturals. Of course, we felt most comfortable around wolves because we were part of them—but we still had the best interests of all in our hearts.

"I'm taking her downstairs before she gets even stronger." Julius clutched my arm and dragged me toward the door.

Something inside me popped as the tingling grew warm—it reminded me of when fur sprouted across my body, but inside me instead. I tried to move my hands to rub the spot, but the handcuffs restrained them.

He hissed but didn't release his hold. Instead, he yanked

harder, causing my feet to drag. I had to get my shit together if I was going to make it out of this. Maybe the connection I felt was because he was a silver wolf like me, and not because he was actually part of my family? It felt similar to my pack bond, but more intense. Maybe because he was one of the last of our kind?

Pushing the horrible thoughts away, I managed to steady my feet underneath me. If I played off like I was pathetic, this guy would know; I had to come across as strong...but not too strong. Hopefully, he'd think I was weaker due to being female—his followers thought that way, so maybe that was a reflection of him.

A large, one-story brick house sat about a hundred yards ahead. It was easily twice the size of Griffin's, which wasn't small to begin with. As we reached the front door, I could see around the edge of the house and saw that there were at least ten cars parked at the side.

This had to be their home base, which meant the rescue mission just got trickier. The sun was beginning its descent from the midday point, which told me it was shortly after noon.

"One wrong move and I'll make you regret it," Julius promised, as we reached the door. "You may be strong, but between me, the bear shifter, and all my men inside, you won't make it far. Silver wolf or not."

He was expecting me to fight but, right now, it was more important for me to focus on every single detail I could. I needed to absorb everything and relay good intel to Griffin... and form a plan of escape in case it came down to me having to get myself the hell out of here. "Noted," I snapped.

We reached the large wraparound porch, and he swung open the oak door and pushed me inside. We entered a gleaming, high-ceilinged foyer that led into a modern living room, confirming my suspicions. This house must have been built in the last ten years.

The walls were a light gray that seemed more commercial than homey. The natural wood floors made the room seem even brighter. There were two large, dark-gray couches in front of a flat-screen television centered on one wall. Other than that, the room was bare; I guessed that only men lived here.

No one else was in the room, and some of the tension in my body slackened. Maybe there were only three of them, after all.

"You're not getting the lay of the land," he said, as he jerked me across the living room to a door in the center of the wall, to the left of the television.

The door swung open, revealing narrow stairs that led down to a basement. Not bothering to turn on the lights, he pushed me forward, making me stumble a few steps down the stairs.

Somehow, I managed not to fall, even though I didn't have my hands at my disposal. I took the first few steps fast, trying to maintain my balance.

He followed closely behind. "You're more nimble than I expected."

That was why he was yanking and pushing me along—he was gauging my capabilities. I should've realized that, but I had been too shocked by his existence and had let him get the best of me.

Again.

How did this asshole keep getting the upper hand? My connection to him pulsed and nagged at me. I wasn't sure what was causing it, but it needed to stop. I didn't want any sort of bond with this monster who was shoving me into a basement so some douchebag could come and force me to be his breeder.

My stomach roiled.

Babe, what's wrong? Griffin linked, and his anxiety mixed with mine.

I would never shut down our bond, but I did try to even out my emotions so he wouldn't feel the turmoil that brewed inside me. That was an alpha tip Dad had given me growing up. Our mates could feel our emotions and could be overwhelmed by them when we lost control of our own minds.

That problem had been steadily increasing since I got here—and by losing focus, I'd given Julius more control. *Other than being led into a basement by a silver wolf who might be my not-so-dead twin brother, nothing,* I tried to joke...but it fell incredibly flat. I should've just given him an update.

What? His voice was girl-shriek level through our link. *We're getting you now.*

No, not yet. I wanted to get out of here and away from Julius, but we couldn't be rash.

Rash would get us killed.

He laughed hysterically. *Not yet? There's no way we aren't.*

Just give me five minutes. I took a deep breath as I approached the bottom of the stairs. I focused on calming myself so I wouldn't upset him more than he already was. *Let me see what we're up against. There are a ton of cars out front. If you come in here and we're outnumbered, then our worst fear will come true: I won't get out of here.*

This is what I was afraid of. His anger and concern grew thick between us. *That we won't be able to get you out. We just handed you over to them without a fucking fight.*

He had every right to be upset. We'd been put in an awful situation. When I thought about the fate of my pack, so much hate rumbled inside me. *I know, but we're going to get out of this.* I refused to accept any other option. *We're going to get through it and stay alive. Is Rosemary with you?*

Yes, and she said the same thing. He growled, not pleased. *That she saw a ton of vehicles when she did her fly-by, and that we needed to wait. There's a crow on the lookout, too. She was almost spotted.*

That confirmed what I'd already suspected. *We're going to have to do the escape at night; otherwise, if there is a bird watching, they'll be alerted since they can see excellently during the day. I'll also be at my strongest, since it's a full moon.* I hadn't wanted to remind him of that last night because he'd have wanted to know why I thought I had to be at my strongest. All it would've done was add more worry.

Yeah, she said the same thing.

When I took the next step, the entire basement came into view. My stomach swooped and churned with nausea. A group of five men were sitting around a table on the right, and straight ahead were two rows of what looked to be six open, barred jail cells with a walkway in the middle.

One of them had a person in it.

"So, this is the girl that you've been obsessing over?" One of the burly men's dark-chocolate eyes perused me as he leaned back in his chair and bounced his foot. His grassy bear scent was strong. "I mean...she's hot, so I get it, but you two look like you could be siblings."

"So, what I'm hearing you say is that you think Julius is attractive too." I ran my mouth, wanting to get under both of their skins. Just as Julius had tested me, I needed to see what I was working with.

"You stupid bitch," the bear sneered, his mouth gaping open with a crazed smile that reminded me of a hyena. "You got a mouth on you. Maybe I should teach you some manners." He stood and rolled his shoulders like he was preparing to hurt me.

"Don't touch her," Julius spoke low and menacing.

Wait. Was he actually protecting me?

I must not have een the only one surprised by his reaction.

A wolf shifter leaned forward across the table, placing his elbows down. He wasn't as large as Julius but was similar to Killian in size. His butterscotch hair hung in his eyes a little, resembling a llama. "Since when do you care if we bust up the prisoners?"

"I don't," Julius barked, as he shoved me again. "But I have someone picking her up tomorrow, and she can't be beat-up, or we won't get paid for the job."

Not bothering to pay attention to the others, I glanced at the prisoner we passed. He looked like a younger version of Carter with the same shaggy brown hair and moss eyes. It must be Randall. The only difference between them was that he seemed stronger than his brother. A bruise circled one of his eyes, making the iris seem brighter.

Great, this was going to be fun. *So, we need to plan on rescuing Carter's brother, too.*

I love that you want to save people. Griffin didn't sound like he loved it at all. *But we have no clue where he is, and we know where you are.*

We do know where he is. I'm looking right at him. He's in the basement with me—in a cage.

Of course, he is. Griffin sounded defeated. *And you won't leave without him.*

I hadn't even considered the possibility, but now that he said it, I realized he was right. *Yeah, pretty much.*

Choosing to divert the conversation, I pressed forward. *There are five large guards down here. One is a bear shifter, and the other four are wolves. That's in addition to the bear shifter and the other wolf who are stationed out front, keeping an eye out for you.*

Rosemary saw at least ten men in the woods before she noticed the bird. He paused. *I want to rush in and get you now, but Rosemary and Killian won't budge. They're threatening to tie me up.*

We're outnumbered. Once again. I was sick of getting into these situations—but at least, having fewer people allowed us to be more flexible. We could hide more. However, having a pack link between all of us would be even more helpful. Something we needed to figure out when this was over with. *We're going to need the darkness.*

Fine, I'll tell the others. Warmth spread through the bond as he said, *I love you.*

I love you too. I pushed back my feelings toward him.

Julius unlocked the cell across from Randall's and pointed inside. "Get in there now. And no funny business. I've got to patrol the area."

Once I was locked in the cell, he spun on his heel and walked back up the stairs, leaving us down here.

ONCE AGAIN, time moved at a snail's pace. There was no visual indication of it passing because we were underground—but the moon was close to rising.

My blood told me that.

Ignoring the pain in my wrists, I sat on the floor of the

prison. I hung my head down, pretending to be defeated for the five guards who glanced my way and snickered, from time to time. I'd named the other three. The one with dark-auburn hair who kept reaching for a red solo cup, made the obvious choice, Solo. Then, the sandy blond guy who kept picking his nose with his left hand became Leftie. And the last guy, fidgeting in his seat the entire time, was dubbed Twitcher.

I ignored them and considered all I knew about Julius. I hated that he knew things about me that other wolves wouldn't. Of course, the best way to hunt a silver wolf was with another one, but who the hell was he? My pack had been the only one of our kind, so I could think of only two options; they'd been swirling inside my head, creating chaos, because one of them wasn't plausible.

The most logical one would be my uncle, who ran. He must have run for a reason—and maybe working with assholes was his motive. But Julius was too young to be my uncle, which left two options but, with the similar features to Mom, really only one viable one.

He was my brother.

The very one who supposedly died at birth—which meant the witch had lied to my parents and kidnapped a member of our family. But why?

However, the *why* didn't matter at the moment. I had to get out of here and take Randall with me, but I couldn't alert him to anything without tipping off the guards.

I had too much damn time to think, and it wasn't good. My wolf itched to take action, and I along with her.

Footsteps pounded down the stairs in Julius's leisurely rhythm. Others probably didn't notice that he purposely walked that way—pretending to be calm for the masses—as any leader would do when they were worried or scared.

"Something wrong, boss?" Hyena, the bear shifter, asked as Julius reached the bottom.

"No." His words were clipped. "But the cavalry is pulling in shortly. They're showing up early to take her." He nodded at me as he headed over. "It's time for you to learn your place in the world."

They're here. I linked with my mate, not able to keep my panic hidden. *Randall and I gotta get out now or never.*

CHAPTER TWENTY-ONE

Once Julius's fingers bit into my arm, our connection strengthened and snapped between us even more. I tried not to focus on that, which was easier than it might have been, because I was damn tired of being manhandled. The raw rage hit me so hard that my skin began to tingle, alerting me to how close I was to shifting. I had to force myself to stay passive so I could surprise them when I needed to. I might have been stronger than any one of them, but even with the full moon's charge, taking down six men would be a challenge.

"But I thought the moon—" Hyena's face scrunched in confusion, making him resemble a bulldog.

"Apparently, they don't care," Julius bit as he dragged me to the stairs. "They say they're prepared and can handle her. They want to bring her to some witch to cut the mate bond before that alpha dumbass gets a read on her." Something like hesitation wafted off him.

The bond between us grew stronger, almost in pace with the moon charging through our blood. A warm spot in my chest formed, but not completely—almost as if something hindered it. The silver moon amplified all our magic, including the link we now had with one another. Whether Julius and I wanted to face the truth about our connection or not, the choice was being taken from us.

Fate always forced her hand.

I used to think that it was poetic. That destiny was mapped out for us. That our lives served a specific purpose. Some wolves liked to complain about their decisions being predetermined by a manipulative bitch—their job, their ranking, their mate—but I refused to think of it that way.

In my mind, fate knew the decisions I would make... almost like foresight. They were my decisions—she just helped solidify the plan for me.

A helping hand.

But for the first time ever, I understood the manipulative bitch sentiment. Because I would've never chosen my pack being slaughtered, my potentially dead brother still being alive, and a constant threat that wanted to ruin my mate bond and use me for their own corrupt desires.

His hand gripped my arm harder, like he wanted to virtually cut the connection off at my skin. Under normal circumstances, I'd have been pissed, but right now, I welcomed the pain. It helped me focus on something other than our bond and my anger.

In other words, it kept my wolf in check.

"Follow me." Julius snapped his fingers with his free hand. "I want all of you up there in case something goes down. Those idiots who are picking her up aren't trained, and there's no telling if they were followed. Another reason they were supposed to wait until tomorrow."

Some of my anxiety ebbed. At least Carter might not be blamed for Killian and Griffin following me. After all, he was only trying to protect his family.

"Angus, take the lead." Julius gestured at Hyena. "Make sure nothing looks funny. The others are probably running their mouths instead of keeping an eye out."

"Yes, sir." He walked in front of me and took the stairs two at a time.

He was an eager one. He must be hoping for a fight. Men like that enjoyed the rush that only fists could achieve and looked forward to inflicting harm on others.

Silver wolves naturally sought out peaceful solutions to conflict. We chose war only when absolutely necessary.

Well, every silver wolf I knew besides Julius. But that glimmer of light inside of him had to be the ways of the silver wolf attempting to influence him.

"Get your ass up those stairs now," he said threateningly. "Or I'll push you up them."

"Shouldn't he come too?" I gestured to Randall.

He pushed me toward the stairs. "No. Now move."

Dammit. I had to think of a way to get Randall out of the basement, but nothing was coming to me.

At least, I could tell that my growing connection with Julius was getting to him. I could sense a portion of his feelings. Not like I could with Griffin, but stronger than a pack bond. Hell, I had no clue what was happening. But the more unsure Julius felt, the edgier he became, which meant he was unpredictable.

And dangerous.

Unpredictability was the thing Dad taught me to be wary of the most. Opponents like that were either unsure how they felt or were completely unhinged. Sometimes, they were one and the same.

I had a feeling Julius was the latter. He wanted to keep his emotions in check, and right now, they were riding a tidal wave, pulling him under.

A feeling I understood all too well—but I had my father's teachings whispering in my mind. He anchored me even in death. Who knew whose teachings were going through Julius's head.

Rosemary killed the crow, so we're making our way in right now. Griffin had a calmness to him that I hadn't felt since last night. *We're getting your ass in the car and taking you home.*

Ah... Taking action appeased him. I put a foot on the first step, moving slowly but steadily. I didn't want to stall so much that I made Julius suspicious, but I wanted to give Griffin and the others as much time as possible to reach me. If Julius got me into the next car, there'd be no going back.

I could feel it in my bones.

Deaths would be rampant, and the thought of who might be willing to die to save me didn't sit well in my stomach. If anything happened to Griffin, it would kill me. Even injury or death to Killian, Sierra, and Rosemary would hurt like losing a pack member.

All of those walls I'd been determined to keep intact had crumbled all around me. Not only had I let Griffin in, but the other three as well.

Julius huffed. "Get your ass moving, *now*." He shoved between my shoulder blades, forcing me to fall forward. My hands were still cuffed behind me, so my chin hit the steps; the pain shot through my jaw and teeth. I had to get out of these handcuffs. I'd been moving my fingers constantly, trying to help keep my blood flowing. Being able to move my hands comfortably to fight as soon as I broke free would be necessary for our survival.

The copper taste of blood filled my mouth, making the smell twice as strong. My stomach roiled as I got on my knees and slowly stood again. "You push me like that one more time, and I'll kick your ass." Just because he couldn't handle our connection didn't mean he got to be a bigger bully and asshole than he already was. I could be complaisant, but I refused to be his punching bag.

"Oh, really?" He snorted. "What are you going to do about it?"

Yeah, okay. I was close to the top of the stairs, and he was being cocky as hell. *Please tell me you guys are ready. I'm about to kick someone's ass.*

What do you mean? Anger laced each one of Griffin's words.

Forcing myself not to turn, I took another step toward the main floor. There were only three steps left until I reached the top, and the front door was only about twenty-five feet from there. I could be outside in less than a minute. *How long until you get here?* I didn't have time to answer all his questions. It was time for action.

We're almost there. Killian and Rosemary are taking out two wolves who were running the perimeter. Sierra and I are coming through the woods in front of the house. A Suburban just arrived with at least four additional guards.

Okay, so they were pretty much in position. None of the wolves here were alarmed, which meant the two Rosemary and Killian were attacking either weren't part of the same pack or they'd taken them down before they could alert anyone. Either option was fine with me as long as no one was aware that an attack had already begun. *I'm kicking ass, starting now. I'll be running out the front door soon.*

I spun around and kicked Julius in the stomach, channeling my wolf and alpha power.

His eyes widened in shock as he fell backward. He reminded me of a bowling ball taking down pins as he tumbled against the guards behind him. All five of them slammed down the stairs, and I pivoted toward the door, taking the last three stairs in one leap.

As I landed on the main floor, I tugged power from the moon and jerked apart my wrists, shattering the handcuffs that had bound me.

"How the hell did you do that?" Hyena's mouth dropped as he stared at the shattered metal on the ground.

"A full moon is rising." I gestured out the window where the moon peeked between the trees. It was twilight, just when the sun and the moon swapped spotlights.

The dumbass turned to see if I spoke the truth, turning his back to me.

Maybe these guys weren't as well trained as I thought. That would be beneficial.

I charged at him before he could spin back around, elbowing him hard on the neck. He dropped and grasped his neck in pain.

However, he didn't go down as I'd hoped. Instead, he rolled his neck like he was working out a kink and lowered his body. Then he ran straight at me.

Hunkering down, I braced for impact. I forced myself to wait until he was about a foot away before moving into action; I didn't want to give away my plan. I pivoted, bringing up my leg and then snapping my foot out to kick him in the stomach. His weight almost knocked me over, but my wolf surged, harnessing my strong magic. His body flew into the wall behind him, and he dropped, groaning.

Footsteps raced up the stairs toward me. Now I had to get the hell out of here. I swung the front door open and paused.

Six men turned toward me. Frosted Tips, Scrawny, and

four new enemies dressed like the men who'd attacked my pack that day. All in black and with ski masks.

Scrawny blinked and shook his head. "That shouldn't be possible."

"Well, it is, dickwad," Frosted Tips growled. He grabbed a pistol from his back pocket and pointed the barrel at me. "But it ends now. One wrong move, and I'll shoot your ass." He shook his head as he chuckled. "Dumb bitch."

Rosemary swooped silently into view and dove toward Frosted Tips.

She was going to be able to attack before they saw her.

A shriek filled the air as Rosemary caught Frosted Tips and lifted him into the sky.

"They've found her!" the shortest of the four new additions yelled, his voice sounding like a toddler's. "Everyone get your guns!"

Every single one of these idiots liked to state the obvious —like, if they didn't say it out loud, no one would know what to do. No wonder they'd had to surprise-attack my pack in the middle of the day of a new moon cycle with machine guns in order to win. We would have slaughtered them otherwise.

"Put me down!" Frosted Tips yelled. They were at least a hundred yards high at that point.

"Gladly." Rosemary retorted, and released him.

The phrase "he screamed like a girl" had never made much sense to me until this moment. The bear shifter sounded like a five-year-old throwing a tantrum over a Barbie doll.

A sickening *crack* sounded as Frosted Tip's body made impact. It bounced a little and a *thump* sounded as the body caved in on itself. Blood spilled from his mouth and eyes, but his death had been immediate. There was no sound of a heartbeat.

I'd never seen anything more disgusting in my life.

"Holy shit," a taller guy in black said, his voice so deep it sounded like a bass guitar.

A gunshot rang out, and Toddler Boy in black grunted as he dropped. Blood puddled under his head from where he'd been shot between the eyes.

The other three men in black pulled guns from their holsters. This was going to be another bloodbath—the very thing I'd hoped to prevent by coming here. Obviously, good intentions didn't matter. Death was inevitable whenever I was involved.

Julius and the four men from the basement barreled out the front door with their guns already in hand. Hyena gimped after them, rubbing his neck and the back of his head with his face fixed in a grimace. His pupils were dilated, meaning he had a concussion.

Once again, we were outnumbered, which seemed to be the norm lately.

Another shot made its mark as Bass Guitar moaned and clutched his shoulder. The bullet hadn't landed a kill shot, and I guessed it must have come from Killian or Sierra.

"Get her now," Julius screamed and pointed at me. "Make sure she stays alive, or all of our asses are toast."

If I could make it to the woods, I would be able to shift and be more helpful. But Julius's four men ran right at me as the three remaining black-clothed guards shot back at my friends.

Julius lifted his gun skyward, pointing at Rosemary.

Normally, I'd have been worried, but I remembered from that night in the woods that Rosemary was able to use her wings to shield us from bullets. She would be fine; it was the others I had to worry about. These men didn't care about killing them.

Griffin, Killian, and Sierra kept shooting, distracting all but Twitcher.

Twitcher made the first move, swinging a punch aimed for my face. I dropped and spun, kicking him in the stomach.

Stumbling back, he gripped his middle and his nostrils flared.

Solo moved to attack, but Twitcher rasped, "Stand down. She's mine." His breathing became labored as he straightened and took slow, deliberate strides toward me. "You're going to pay for that," he threatened.

"Come at me," I smirked, channeling my crazed side. "Back up those idle threats with some worthy action," I wanted to make him mad and embarrassed that a woman had mocked him. Taking him down would be so much sweeter.

"Keep it up," he spat. "I'm going to make you beg for forgiveness."

"Oh, wait." I'd always thought Dad had exaggerated the standard male alpha elitist, as if trying to purposely enrage me. The sad truth was he hadn't at all. We were stuck in an old hierarchy where women were expected to submit and obey. Boy, did I have a lesson to teach them all. "You kidnapped me and held me against my will, and I'm supposed to be the one who begs?" I lifted my hand and gestured for him to come on. "Bring it, prick, so I can put you in your place. But unlike me, you'll be crying for mercy. Don't waste your breath asking for forgiveness."

Gunshots fired, and the three guys in black ran toward the tree line, while Scrawny turned and ran down the driveway toward the main road.

Julius shot at Rosemary, and as expected, she blocked the bullets, but couldn't get any closer since she had to use her wings for protection and not flying.

Unfortunately, the angle of the house and our positions meant my allies didn't have a clear shot at Julius or the four assholes surrounding me.

I was on my own. At least, for now. I had to figure out a way to give us the advantage—but we were outgunned. I needed to take down these four clowns so I could help the others.

Leftie was at least three times my size. He hissed and ran toward me, no doubt planning to use the force of his weight against me. There was no room for error. One misstep, and he'd have me right where he wanted me.

CHAPTER TWENTY-TWO

"Augh," Leftie grunted as he lunged, aiming for my body.

I dropped to the ground on my back. As he flew over me, I kicked him in the nuts and lifted him, causing him to flip over and land on *his* back.

A loud thud and groan confirmed that I'd hit my mark.

I climbed back up and into a fighter's stance with my feet shoulder-width apart, shuffling backward to keep an eye on everything going on around me while I moved into sight of Griffin and the others.

If I wanted their help, I had to position myself so they could see me *and* my attackers.

Leftie rolled over and vomited chunky bits of whatever he'd eaten; the stench stole my breath away. My own stomach rolled like it wanted to sympathy barf beside him.

Yeah, not happening. I breathed through my mouth and kept my eyes averted from him. He'd be down for a while.

The firing stopped, and the other three descended on me. They weren't underestimating me as the other two had.

"Watch her," Hyena warned, and rubbed his neck. "She's stronger than she looks."

"Yeah, dumbasses." Llama smirked. "She's a fucking silver wolf. What did you expect? You've fought Julius."

"But he's a man." Hyena waved a hand toward me. "She's less than half his size, but she delivers a stronger punch."

Dammit. I'd fooled them at first, but the ruse was over. They were aware of what I could do...granted, they didn't know to what extent. I smiled, hoping I looked crazed. If they were attacking me in groups now, then they were at least a little nervous, so I needed to play into it.

Act deranged.

I forced laughter from deep inside my belly while shaking my head. The sound chafed my throat due to the anxiety mixed within it. As much as they were scared, so was I. Not only for myself, but for my friends.

I was so tired of putting us all in danger.

My blood pumped with the moon's magic. I took a second to glance in its direction, noting that it was above the trees now. The light shone on me, giving me a silver moon high.

Raising my hands, I watched my skin glisten silver. On nights like these, I could take on the world.

"Dude, her skin and eyes..." Solo sounded awed. "I've never seen anything like that before."

Wait. If they'd been around Julius, then they should've seen this before now. I glanced at the other silver wolf and noticed a faint hint of silver around him, but nothing like my alpha shimmer, or even like my pack members had. Alpha blood contained the strongest magic, and thus, Dad and I always looked more silver than the others—but they'd still shone brightly in the moonlight.

Maybe he wasn't my brother, after all.

The thought both comforted and upset me. I didn't need a family member who was out for my blood, but at the same time, having any sort of family would be nice...even a cousin. I understood that Griffin was my family now, but he couldn't understand the struggles of being a silver wolf. No matter how hard he might try, he would never fully get there, just like Mom.

"What are you doing?" Julius yelled, turning to face us. "She's leading you right in front of her friends. Get her ass back over there." He glanced at Rosemary, who was swooping toward us again, and fired a few rounds, stalling her. He shoved me back toward the front door, where Griffin and the others didn't have a clear view of me anymore. However, when his hand touched me, the warm spot in my chest solidified as our bond snapped into place.

His conflicting feelings slammed into me almost as powerfully as Griffin's. He inhaled sharply, and his gunfire halted as he shifted his entire focus to severing the connection between us.

Solo, Llama, and Twitcher descended on me like I was the prey they desperately needed.

Llama moved behind me and clutched my arms like he could restrain them permanently behind me. I played along and leaned back against him as Solo pulled out another set of handcuffs—as if those could hold me.

They hadn't seen what I'd done to the other pair. They'd been downstairs.

As Solo got closer, I leaned back on Llama and kicked Solo in the jaw. He twisted through the air and landed several feet away, his head hitting the ground with a sickening crack.

"Don't waste your time with handcuffs," Hyena said as

he bounded off the porch, already recovered enough to join the fight. "'The bitch shattered the other ones."

I was tired of being bullied and called derogatory names just because I was female. I pulled more power from the moon, making myself even stronger. I leaned forward and threw Llama over my body. His hold released as he tried to catch his fall, but he landed hard on his back, hitting his head and passing out.

"Julius," Twitcher shouted. "She's kicking our asses."

Dammit, are you okay? Griffin linked.

Yeah. I glanced in his direction for a second and could just make out the three of them squatting in the tree line. *How about you guys?*

We're trying to get to you. He sounded frustrated. *We hit another one of them.*

I'll be there to help in a second. It was time to end this.

Not wanting to be on the defensive any longer, I decided to take control of the situation. I no longer had any reason to not go all out. I called to my wolf, asking for her to come forward. She gladly obliged, and within seconds, my bones began to crack and reform. Before long, I was on four legs, completely shifted into my animal form.

"Holy shit." Hyena stopped and stared.

On nights like these, my wolf was huge; on all four legs, I was the same height as I was in human form. I bared my teeth and stalked toward Hyena, letting him know that he was the prey, not me.

His bottom lip quivered as he seemed to realize he was on the wrong side...at least, at the moment.

That wasn't going to win him sympathy. He'd proven that he had no remorse about handing me off to a horrible fate. The only reason he had regret now was because of his fear.

As if realizing his best chance of survival was in his animal form, he began his own shift.

I'd never fought a bear before, so this would be interesting. More hair sprouted along his body even though I wasn't sure how. The asshole had been hairy as fuck, to begin with.

He roared at me in his beast form.

However, he didn't have the size advantage he would on standard wolves—because I was the same size. He barreled toward me, probably planning on using his brute strength against me. I easily dodged him, and he ran past me several feet before he could stop. He skidded in the gravel and spun back around.

Drool dripped from his teeth as his chest heaved. He lumbered back in my direction but, this time, didn't race like before. He anticipated that I'd dodge him again. So, when he got close, he stood on his back two legs and wrapped his arms around my body, countering my move.

He'd surprised me...and it infuriated me. I'd been trained better than that.

As he tightened his hold, pain coursed through my body, alerting Griffin.

Sterlyn. Griffin cried through our bond.

I'm fine. If he did something stupid, then both of us would get hurt. There was no way in hell I'd let anything happen to him. *He doesn't have me.*

As Hyena wrapped his arms around me, I sank my teeth into his upper shoulder.

He grunted as he stumbled back and then attacked again, swiping a paw at me. I tried to get out of the way, but his claws slashed into my leg. Pain radiated, but luckily, I'd gotten out of the way enough that it wasn't detrimental—only a minor inconvenience, since I could heal quickly under the Silver Moon.

Not wanting him to gain the upper hand, I lunged at his neck. He swung an arm, swatting me like a fly. I flew back several feet and landed on my side. Fighting through the ache, I forced myself back onto all fours.

Hyena scuffed his paws in the gravel, throwing out small rocks and dirt that hit my face and legs. The rocks stung, but the dirt in my eyes was the bigger concern.

Dammit, he was fighting dirty. Of course, he was.

I closed my eyes and focused solely on hearing as heavy paws pounded my way. Hyena was running at me at an angle. At the very last second, I dropped and rolled in the opposite direction, forcing him to fall with a thud. I then jumped on his back and sank my teeth into his uninjured shoulder.

Growling, he bucked like a bull in a rodeo, trying to fling me from his back—but I dug my teeth in deeper, along with my claws. I shredded the skin all along his back, and he whimpered in pain. Eventually, he dropped and rolled, capturing me under his weight.

For a second, I couldn't breathe, but it was just my mind playing tricks on me. Getting my head on straight, I stretched, reaching the side of his neck. That was all I needed. I bit down right where the artery was. Even though I wasn't fully ripping out his throat, he'd bleed out too quickly to heal this way. It wasn't an instant death, but it wouldn't take long.

Blood poured from his wound, coating the fur around my neck and chest crimson. He lurched to his feet as if he thought that would reverse the fatality of the injury. Within a few steps, his legs gave out, and he succumbed to the inevitable.

Not worried about him anymore, I turned my attention

to find Llama back on his feet. He'd been trying to sneak up on me while I'd been preoccupied with Hyena.

His eyes widened, and he shook his head and raised his hands. "Look, I don't mean to cause any trouble."

But that wasn't the truth, according to the horrible stench swirling around. Everyone here had a darkness within them that told me otherwise. And, unlike Julius, they didn't seem to have any redeeming sensibilities. They'd be after me again in a heartbeat. Hell, to be fair, Julius probably would be, too.

"Don't be a damn pussy." Leftie climbed to his feet, his face red with either pain or rage. Most likely a combination of the two.

My natural instinct was to focus on Leftie, but Llama had proven he had no problem trying to attack me while I was preoccupied. Since he was pretending to surrender, I couldn't force myself to kill him, but I could knock his ass out.

Using the element of surprise, I kicked at his head, forcing his body to spin hard to the ground.

Leftie said with disgust, "That asshole deserved it."

Not wanting to hear any more of his lip, I lowered my head and bulldozed him, past Julius—who was still shooting at Rosemary—and five feet away into the trees where Griffin and Killian were located.

Leftie tried to get a grip around my neck, but his hands slipped on the fresh blood. I picked up my pace and slammed his body into a tree trunk, and his arms jerked with an accompanying *crack*. When I stepped back, his body crumpled at my feet. I realized that I must have broken his neck, and his heart wasn't beating any longer.

I spun back around to locate Twitcher, only to see him

racing down the gravel road. One of the men dressed in black growled and shot at him, and he cried out as he fell.

"You know there is no escape," Bass Guitar yelled at him. "Now you're going to wish you'd died."

I imagined they planned on beating the shit out of him, and God knew what else. No wonder the first bear shifter to kidnap me had killed himself that day.

Rosemary landed beside me, her twilight eyes filled with worry. She touched my fur, and her power entered me, but after a few seconds, she sighed with relief.

My heart raced with fear from her being here since she'd been fighting Julius. However, I could feel the connection still between me and Julius, and I turned to find him lying still on the ground. My body tensed, then sagged with relief when I realized he was breathing.

She must have understood because she wiped the blood from her hands onto her pants and sighed. "I was told to protect the silver wolves no matter what."

She'd told me that before—and I realized it applied to Julius, too. The weight that lifted from my shoulders once I understood that told me I already cared about this man more than I should. The connection between us *was* familial.

I nodded and focused on my next few targets. Once we eliminated them, we could get the hell out of here.

Rosemary ran next to me, pointing to the man on the far right, and gestured at herself. Then, she motioned at the one on the left and at me. The message was clear. We'd get the two on the outside, and Bass Guitar, who was in the center, was already hurt and not able to react quickly; because of his injured shoulder, he wouldn't be able to train his gun in opposite directions, so when he turned to shoot at Rosemary, I could take his ass down. They wouldn't shoot at me first since they were supposed to keep me alive.

Moving as quietly as possible, I trotted toward the man on the left. Of course, that was the moment that the breeze changed directions and blew my scent his way. He tensed and pivoted toward me. His attention flicked to the bodies that lay scattered around, and then to the angel who was about to attack his cohort.

"How the hell do you all keep doing this?" he asked, his voice thick with anger. "We were told if we couldn't take you alive, we should kill you on the spot." He pulled out his gun and aimed it right at me. I pushed my legs, trying to reach him before he could fire.

The mixture of my parents' scents invaded my senses... almost as if I was trying to remember them one last time before I died. Panic sank deep inside me and seeped through the bond connecting me and Julius. But that didn't make sense. He was passed out behind me.

Griffin's cry filled my ears as gunfire went crazy, and I linked to him. *I love you.*

Rosemary flapped toward me, her hand reaching out for me.

The sound of a gunshot echoed loud, and a flash of silver slammed into me as Julius's voice popped into my head, *No! She can't die.*

I landed hard, my breath knocked out of me by either the force of the impact or the fact that we had some sort of bond that now allowed him to mind-link with me. Julius held me down, his face set with pure determination.

Gunshots rang from Bass Guitar and his two friends, back in the direction of Griffin and the others. So, when Griffin reached my side and shoved Julius off me, I couldn't believe my eyes. I had to be imagining him in my final moments alive—but I didn't care as the mirage pulled me into his arms, tears running down his face.

Grateful to be with my mate, I focused on what had just happened between Julius and me. *But how?* I linked to Julius, even though my mind was reeling from everything else. I wasn't sure what I was addressing—him saving me or talking in my mind. Our eyes locked as some sort of battle sprang up between us like our wolves were fighting to dominate one another.

Was it that important to him to get paid and hand me over to whoever had hired him?

It didn't matter.

He'd soon regret saving me from that bullet...because our fight had just begun.

ABOUT THE AUTHOR

Jen L. Grey is a *USA Today* Bestselling Author who writes Paranormal Romance, Urban Fantasy, and Fantasy genres.

Jen lives in Tennessee with her husband, two daughters, and two miniature Australian Shepherd. Before she began writing, she was an avid reader and enjoyed being involved in the indie community. Her love for books eventually led her to writing. For more information, please visit her website and sign up for her newsletter.

Check out my future projects and book signing events at my website.
www.jenlgrey.com

ALSO BY JEN L. GREY

Shadow City: The Silver Wolf

Broken Mate

Rising Darkness

Silver Moon

The Hidden King Trilogy

Dragon Mate

Dragon Heir

Dragon Queen

The Wolf Born Trilogy

Hidden Mate

Blood Secrets

Awakened Magic

The Marked Wolf Trilogy

Moon Kissed

Chosen Wolf

Broken Curse

Wolf Moon Academy Trilogy

Shadow Mate

Blood Legacy

Rising Fate

The Royal Heir Trilogy

Wolves' Queen

Wolf Unleashed

Wolf's Claim

Bloodshed Academy Trilogy

Year One

Year Two

Year Three

The Half-Breed Prison Duology (Same World As Bloodshed Academy)

Hunted

Cursed

The Artifact Reaper Series

Reaper: The Beginning

Reaper of Earth

Reaper of Wings

Reaper of Flames

Reaper of Water

Stones of Amaria (Shared World)

Kingdom of Storms

Kingdom of Shadows

Kingdom of Ruins

Kingdom of Fire

The Pearson Prophecy

Dawning Ascent

Enlightened Ascent

Reigning Ascent

Stand Alones

Death's Angel

Rising Alpha

CPSIA information can be obtained
at www.ICGtesting.com
Printed in the USA
LVHW100208021222
734458LV00016B/79